Arthur Helps

Friends in Council

Volume 1

Arthur Helps

Friends in Council
Volume 1

ISBN/EAN: 9783337301743

Printed in Europe, USA, Canada, Australia, Japan

Cover: Foto ©Andreas Hilbeck / pixelio.de

More available books at **www.hansebooks.com**

CASSELL'S NATIONAL LIBRARY.

FRIENDS IN COUNCIL.

First Series.

BY

SIR ARTHUR HELPS.

CASSELL & COMPANY, Limited:

LONDON, PARIS & MELBOURNE.

1891.

INTRODUCTION.

ARTHUR HELPS was born at Streatham on the 10th of July, 1813. He went at the age of sixteen to Eton, thence to Trinity College, Cambridge. Having graduated B.A. in 1835, he became private secretary to the Hon. T. Spring Rice, who was Chancellor of the Exchequer in Lord Melbourne's Cabinet, formed in April, 1835. This was his position at the beginning of the present reign in June, 1837.

In 1839—in which year he graduated M.A.— Arthur Helps was transferred to the service of Lord Morpeth, who was Irish Secretary in the same ministry. Lord Melbourne's Ministry was succeeded by that of Sir Robert Peel in September, 1841, and Helps then was appointed a Commissioner of French, Danish, and Spanish Claims. In 1841 he published "Essays Written in the Intervals of Business." Their quiet thoughtfulness was in accord with the spirit that had given value to his services as private secretary to two ministers of State. In 1844 that little book was followed by another on "The Claims of Labour," dealing with the relations of employers to employed. There was the same scholarly simplicity and grace of style, the same interest in things worth serious attention. "We say," he wrote, towards the close, "that Kings are God's Vicegerents upon Earth; but almost every human being has, at one time or other of his life, a portion of the happiness of those around him in his power, which might make him tremble, if he did but see it in all its fulness." To this book Arthur Helps added an essay "On the Means of Improving the Health and Increasing the Comfort of the Labouring Classes."

His next book was this First Series of "Friends in Council," published in 1847, and followed by other series in later years. There were many other writings of his, less popular than they would have been if the same abilities had been controlled by less good taste. His "History of the Conquest of the New World" in 1848, and of "The Spanish Conquest of America," in four volumes, from 1855 to 1861, preceded his obtaining from his University, in 1864, the honorary degree of D.C.L. In June, 1860, Arthur Helps was made Clerk of the Privy Council, and held that office of high trust until his death on the 7th of March, 1875. He had become Sir Arthur in 1872.

H. M.

FRIENDS IN COUNCIL.

CHAPTER I.

NONE but those who, like myself, have once lived in intellectual society, and then have been deprived of it for years, can appreciate the delight of finding it again. Not that I have any right to complain, if I were fated to live as a recluse for ever. I can add little, or nothing, to the pleasure of any company; I like to listen rather than to talk; and when anything apposite does occur to me, it is generally the day after the conversation has taken place. I do not, however, love good talk the less for these defects of mine; and I console myself with thinking that I sustain the part of a judicious listener, not always an easy one.

Great, then, was my delight at hearing last year that my old pupil, Milverton, had taken a house which had long been vacant in our neighbourhood. To add to my pleasure, his college friend, Ellesmere, the great lawyer, also an old pupil of mine, came to us frequently in the course of the autumn. Milverton was at that time writing some essays which he occasionally read to Ellesmere and myself. The conversations which then took place I am proud to say that I have chronicled. I think they must be interesting to the world in general, though of course not so much so as to me.

Milverton and Ellesmere were my favourite pupils.

Many is the heartache I have had at finding that those boys, with all their abilities, would do nothing at the University. But it was in vain to urge them. I grieve to say that neither of them had any ambition of the right kind. Once I thought I had stimulated Ellesmere to the proper care and exertion ; when, to my astonishment and vexation, going into his rooms about a month before an examination, I found that, instead of getting up his subjects, like a reasonable man, he was absolutely endeavouring to invent some new method for proving something which had been proved before in a hundred ways. Over this he had wasted two days, and from that moment I saw it was useless to waste any more of my time and patience in urging a scholar so indocile for the beaten path.

What tricks he and Milverton used to play me, pretending not to understand my demonstration of some mathematical problem, inventing all manner of subtle difficulties, and declaring they could not go on while these stumbling-blocks lay in their way ! But I am getting into college gossip, which may in no way delight my readers. And I am fancying, too, that Milverton and Ellesmere are the boys they were to me ; but I am now the child to them. During the years that I have been quietly living here, they have become versed in the ways of the busy world. And though they never think of asserting their superiority, I feel it, and am glad to do so.

My readers would, perhaps, like me to tell them something of the characters of Ellesmere and Milverton ; but it would ill become me to give that insight into them, which I, their college friend and tutor, imagine I have obtained. Their friendship I could never understand. It was not on the surface very warm, and their congeniality seemed to result more from one or two large common principles of thought than from any peculiar similarity of taste, or from great affection on either side. Yet I should wrong their friendship if I were to represent it otherwise than a most true-hearted one; more so, perhaps, than some of softer texture. What needs be seen of them individually will be by their words, which I hope I have in the main retained.

The place where we generally met in fine weather was on the lawn before Milverton's house. It was an eminence which commanded a series of valleys sloping towards the sea. And, as the sea was not more than nine miles off, it was a matter of frequent speculation with us whether the landscape was bounded by air or water. In the first valley was a little town of red brick houses, with poplars coming up amongst them. The ruins of a castle, and some water which, in olden times, had been the lake in "the pleasaunce," were between us and the town. The clang of an anvil, or the clamour of a horn, or busy wheelwright's sounds, came faintly up to us when the wind was south.

I must not delay my readers longer with my gossip, but bring them at once into the conversation that preceded our first reading.

Milverton. I tell you, Ellesmere, these are the only heights I care to look down from, the heights of natural scenery.

Ellesmere. Pooh! my dear Milverton, it is only because the particular mounds which the world calls heights, you think *f*ou have found out to be but larger ant-heaps. Whenever you have cared about anything, a man more fierce and unphilosophical in the pursuit of it I never saw. To influence men's minds by writing for them, is that no ambition ?

Milverton. It may be, but I have it not. Let any kind critic convince me that what I am now doing is useless, or has been done before, or that, if I leave it undone, some one else will do it to my mind; and I should fold up my papers, and watch the turnips grow in that field there, with a placidity that would, perhaps, seem very spiritless to your now restless and ambitious nature, Ellesmere.

Ellesmere. If something were to happen which will not, then—O Philosophy, Philosophy, you, too, are a good old nurse, and rattle your rattles for your little people, as well as old Dame World can do for hers. But what are we to have to-day for our first reading ?

Milverton. An Essay on Truth.

Ellesmere. Well, had I known this before, it is not the novelty of the subject which would have dragged me up the hill to your house. By the way, philosophers ought not to live upon hills. They are much more accessible, and I think quite as reasonable, when, Diogenes-like, they live in tubs upon flat ground. Now for the essay.

TRUTH.

Truth is a subject which men will not suffer to grow old. Each age has to fight with its own falsehoods:

each man with his love of saying to himself and those around him pleasant things and things serviceable for to-day, rather than the things which are. Yet a child appreciates at once the divine necessity for truth; never asks, "What harm is there in saying the thing that is not?" and an old man finds, in his growing experience, wider and wider applications of the great doctrine and discipline of truth.

Truth needs the wisdom of the serpent as well as the simplicity of the dove. He has gone but a little way in this matter who supposes that it is an easy thing for a man to speak the truth, "the thing he troweth;" and that it is a casual function, which may be fulfilled at once after any lapse of exercise. But, in the first place, the man who would speak truth must know what he troweth. To do that, he must have an uncorrupted judgment. By this is not meant a perfect judgment or even a wise one, but one which, however it may be biassed, is not bought—is still a judgment. But some people's judgments are so entirely gained over by vanity, selfishness, passion, or inflated prejudices and fancies long indulged in; or they have the habit of looking at everything so carelessly, that they see nothing truly. They cannot interpret the world of reality. And this is the saddest form of lying, "the lie that sinketh in," as Bacon says, which becomes part of the character and goes on eating the rest away.

Again, to speak truth, a man must not only have that martial courage which goes out, with sound of drum and trumpet, to do and suffer great things; but that domestic courage which compels him to utter small

sounding truths in spite of present inconvenience and
outraged sensitiveness or sensibility. Then he must
not be in any respect a slave to self-interest. Often
it seems as if but a little misrepresentation would gain
a great good for us ; or, perhaps, we have only to
conceal some trifling thing, which, if told, might hinder
unreasonably, as we think, a profitable bargain. The
true man takes care to tell, notwithstanding. When we
think that truth interferes at one time or another with
all a man's likings, hatings, and wishes, we must
admit, I think, that it is the most comprehensive and
varied form of self-denial.

Then, in addition to these great qualities, truth-
telling in its highest sense requires a well-balanced
mind. For instance, much exaggeration, perhaps the
most, is occasioned by an impatient and easily moved
temperament which longs to convey its own vivid
impressions to other minds, and seeks by amplifying to
gain the full measure of their sympathy. But a true
man does not think what his hearers are feeling, but
what he is saying.

More stress might be laid than has been on the
intellectual requisites for truth, which are probably the
best part of intellectual cultivation ; and as much caused
by truth as causing it.* But, putting the requisites
for truth at the fewest, see of how large a portion of
the character truth is the resultant. If you were to
make a list of those persons accounted the religious
men of their respective ages, you would have a ludicrous
combination of characters essentially dissimilar. But

* See *Statesman*, p. 30.

true people are kindred. Mention the eminently true men, and you will find that they are a brotherhood. There is a family likeness throughout them.

If we consider the occasions of exercising truthfulness and descend to particulars, we may divide the matter into the following heads:—truth to oneself—truth to mankind in general—truth in social relations—truth in business—truth in pleasure.

1. Truth to oneself. All men have a deep interest that each man should tell himself the truth. Not only will he become a better man, but he will understand them better. If men knew themselves, they could not be intolerant to others.

It is scarcely necessary to say much about the advantage of a man knowing himself for himself. To get at the truth of any history is good; but a man's own history—when he reads that truly, and, without a mean and over-solicitous introspection, knows what he is about and what he has been about, it is a Bible to him. "And David said unto Nathan, I have sinned before the Lord." David knew the truth about himself. But truth to oneself is not merely truth about oneself. It consists in maintaining an openness and justness of soul which brings a man into relation with all truth. For this, all the senses, if you might so call them, of the soul must be uninjured—that is, the affections and the perceptions must be just. For a man to speak the truth to himself comprehends all goodness; and for us mortals can only be an aim.

2. Truth to mankind in general. This is a matter which, as I read it, concerns only the higher natures. Suffice it to say, that the withholding large truths from the world may be a betrayal of the greatest trust.

3. Truth in social relations. Under this head come the practices of making speech vary according to the person spoken to ; of pretending to agree with the world when you do not ; of not acting according to what is your deliberate and well-advised opinion because some mischief may be made of it by persons whose judgment in this matter you do not respect ; of maintaining a wrong course for the sake of consistency ; of encouraging the show of intimacy with those whom you never can be intimate with ; and many things of the same kind. These practices have elements of charity and prudence as well as fear and meanness in them. Let those parts which correspond to fear and meanness be put aside. Charity and prudence are not parasitical plants which require boles of falsehood to climb up upon. It is often extremely difficult in the mixed things of this world to act truly and kindly too ; but therein lies one of the great trials of man, that his sincerity should have kindness in it, and his kindness truth.

4. Truth in business. The more truth you can get into any business, the better. Let the other side know the defects of yours, let them know how you are to be satisfied, let there be as little to be found as possible (I should say nothing), and if your business be an honest

one, it will be best tended in this way. The talking, bargaining, and delaying that would thus be needless, the little that would then have to be done over again, the anxiety that would be put aside, would even in a worldly way be "great gain." It is not, perhaps, too much to say, that the third part of men's lives is wasted by the effect, direct or indirect, of falsehoods.

Still, let us not be swift to imagine that lies are never of any service. A recent Prime Minister said that he did not know about truth always prevailing and the like; but lies had been very successful against his government. And this was true enough. Every lie has its day. There is no preternatural inefficacy in it by reason of its falseness. And this is especially the case with those vague injurious reports which are no man's lies, but all men's carelessness. But even as regards special and unmistakable falsehood, we must admit that it has its success. A complete being might deceive with wonderful effect; however, as nature is always against a liar, it is great odds in the case of ordinary mortals. Wolsey talks of

> " Negligence
> Fit for a fool to fall by,"

when he gives Henry the wrong packet; but the Cardinal was quite mistaken. That kind of negligence was just the thing of which far-seeing and thoughtful men are capable; and which, if there were no higher motive, should induce them to rely on truth alone. A very close vulpine nature, all eyes, all ears, may succeed better in deceit. But it is a sleepless business. Yet, strange to say, it is had recourse to in the most spend-thrift fashion, as the first and easiest thing that comes to hand.

In connection with truth in business, it may be observed that if you are a truthful man, you should be watchful over those whom you employ ; for your subordinate agents are often fond of lying for your interests, as they think. Show them at once that you do not think with them, and that you will disconcert any of their inventions by breaking in with the truth. If you suffer the fear of seeming unkind to prevent your thrusting well-meant inventions aside, you may get as much pledged to falsehoods as if you had coined and uttered them yourself.

5. Truth in pleasure. Men have been said to be sincere in their pleasures ; but this is only that the taste and habits of men are more easily discernible in pleasure than in business. The want of truth is as great a hindrance to the one as to the other. Indeed, there is so much insincerity and formality in the pleasurable department of human life, especially in social pleasures, that instead of a bloom there is a slime upon it, which deadens and corrupts the thing. One of the most comical sights to superior beings must be to see two human creatures with elaborate speech and gestures making each other exquisitely uncomfortable from civility : the one pressing what he is most anxious that the other should not accept, and the other accepting only from the fear of giving offence by refusal. There is an element of charity in all this too ; and it will be

the business of a just and refined nature to be sincere and considerate at the same time. This will be better done by enlarging our sympathy, so that more things and people are pleasant to us, than by increasing the civil and conventional part of our nature, so that we are able to do more seeming with greater skill and endurance. Of other false hindrances to pleasure, such as ostentation and pretences of all kinds, there is neither charity nor comfort in them. They may be got rid of altogether, and no moaning made over them. Truth, which is one of the largest creatures, opens out the way to the heights of enjoyment, as well as to the depths of self-denial.

It is difficult to think too highly of the merits and delights of truth; but there is often in men's minds an exaggerated notion of some bit of truth, which proves a great assistance to falsehood. For instance, the shame of some particular small falsehood, exaggeration, or insincerity, becomes a bugbear which scares a man into a career of false dealing. He has begun making a furrow a little out of the line, and he ploughs on in it to try and give some consistency and meaning to it. He wants almost to persuade himself that it was not wrong, and entirely to hide the wrongness from others. This is a tribute to the majesty of truth; also to the world's opinion about truth. It proceeds, too, upon the notion that all falsehoods are equal, which is not the case; or on some fond craving for a show of perfection, which is sometimes very inimical to the reality. The practical, as well as the high-minded, view in such cases, is for a man to think how he can be true now. To attain that, it may, even for this world, be worth while for a man to admit that he is inconsistent, and even that he has been untrue. His hearers, did they know anything of themselves, would be fully aware that he was not singular, except in the courage of owning his insincerity.

Ellesmere. That last part requires thinking about. If you were to permit men, without great loss of reputation, to own that they had been insincere, you might break down some of that majesty of truth you talk about. And bad men might avail themselves of any facilities of owning insincerity, to commit more of it. I can imagine that the apprehension of this might restrain a man from making any such admission as you allude to, even if he could make up his mind to do it otherwise.

Milverton. Yes; but can anything be worse than a man going on in a false course? Each man must look to his own truthfulness, and keep that up as well as he can, even at the risk of saying, or doing, something which may be turned to ill account by others. We may think too much about this reflection of our external selves. Let the real self be right. I am not so fanciful as to expect men to go about clamouring that they have been false; but at no risk of letting people see that, or of even being obliged to own it, should they persevere in it.

Dunsford. Milverton is right, I think.

Ellesmere. Do not imagine that I am behind either of you in a wish to hold up truth. My only doubt was as to the mode. For my own part, I have such faith in truth that I take it mere concealment is in most cases a mischief. And I should say, for instance, that a wise man would be sorry that his fellows should think better of him than he deserves. By the way, that is a reason why I should not like to be a writer of moral essays, Milverton—one should be supposed to be so very good.

Milverton. Only by thoughtless people then. There is a saying given to Rousseau, not that he ever did say it, for I believe it was a misprint, but it was a possible saying for him, "Chaque homme qui pense est méchant." Now, without going the length of this aphorism, we may say that what has been well written has been well suffered.

" He best can paint them who has felt them most."

And so, though we should not exactly declare that writers who have had much moral influence have been wicked men, yet we may admit that they have been amongst the most struggling, which implies anything but serene self-possession and perfect spotlessness. If you take the great ones, Luther, Shakespeare, Goethe, you see this at once.

Dunsford. David, St. Paul.

Milverton. Such men are like great rocks on the sea-shore. By their resistance, terraces of level land are formed ; but the rocks themselves bear many scars and ugly indents, while the sea of human difficulty presents the same unwrinkled appearance in all ages. Yet it has been driven back.

Ellesmere. But has it lost any of its bulk, or only gone elsewhere ? One part of the resemblance certainly is that these same rocks, which were bulwarks, become, in their turn, dangers.

Milverton. Yes, there is always loss in that way. It is seldom given to man to do unmixed good. But it was not this aspect of the simile that I was thinking of : it was the scarred appearance.

Dunsford. Scars not always of defeat or flight; scars in the front.

Milverton. Ah, it hardly does for us to talk of victory or defeat, in these cases ; but we may look at the contest itself as something not bad, terminate how it may. We lament over a man's sorrows, struggles, disasters, and shortcomings ; yet they were possessions too. We talk of the origin of evil and the permission of evil. But what is evil ? We mostly speak of sufferings and trials as good, perhaps, in their result ; but we hardly admit that they may be good in themselves. Yet they are knowledge—how else to be acquired, unless by making men as gods, enabling them to understand without experience. All that men go through may be absolutely the best for them—no such thing as evil, at least in our customary meaning of the word. But, you will say, they might have been created different and higher. See where this leads to. Any sentient being may set up the same claim : a fly that it had not been made a man ; and so the end would be that each would complain of not being all.

Ellesmere. Say it all over again, my dear Milverton : it is rather hard. [Milverton did so, in nearly the same words.] I think I have heard it all before. But you may have it as you please. I do not say this irreverently, but the truth is, I am too old and too earthly to enter upon these subjects. I think, however, that the view is a stout-hearted one. It is somewhat in the same vein of thought that you see in Carlyle's works about the contempt of happiness. But in all these cases, one is apt to think of the sage in "Rasselas," who is very wise about human misery till he loses his daughter. Your fly illustration has something in it. Certainly when men talk big about what might have been done for man, they omit to think what might be said, on similar grounds, for each sentient creature in the universe. But here have we been meandering off into origin of evil, and uses of great men, and wickedness of writers, etc., whereas I meant to have said something about the essay. How would you answer what Bacon maintains? "A mixture of a lie doth ever add pleasure."

Milverton. He is not speaking of the lies of social life, but of self-deception. He goes on to class under that head " vain opinions, flattering hopes, false valuations, imaginations as one would." These things are the sweetness of " the lie that sinketh in." Many a man has a kind of mental kaleidoscope, where the bits of broken glass are his own merits and fortunes, and they fall into harmonious arrangements and delight him—often most mischievously and to his ultimate detriment, but they are a present pleasure.

Ellesmere. Well, I am going to be true in my pleasures: to take a long walk alone. I have got a difficult case for an opinion, which I must go and think over.

Dunsford. Shall we have another reading to-morrow?

Milverton. Yes, if you are both in the humour for it.

CHAPTER II.

As the next day was fine, we agreed to have our reading in the same spot that I have described before. There was scarcely any conversation worth noting, until after Milverton had read us the following essay on Conformity.

CONFORMITY.

The conformity of men is often a far poorer thing than that which resembles it amongst the lower animals. The monkey imitates from imitative skill and game-someness: the sheep is gregarious, having no sufficient will to form an independent project of its own. But man often loathes what he imitates, and conforms to what he knows to be wrong.

It will ever be one of the nicest problems for a man to solve how far he shall profit by the thoughts of other men, and not be enslaved by them. He comes into the world, and finds swaddling clothes ready for his mind as well as his body. There is a vast scheme of social machinery set up about him; and he has to discern how he can make it work with him and for him, without becoming part of the machinery himself. In this lie the anguish and the struggle of the greatest minds. Most sad are they, having mostly the deepest sympathies, when they find themselves breaking off from communion with other minds. They would go on, if they could, with the opinions around them. But, happily, there is something to which a man owes a larger allegiance than to any human affection. He would be content to go away from a false thing, or quietly to protest against it ; but in spite of him the strife in his heart breaks into burning utterance by word or deed.

Few, however, are those who venture, even for the shortest time, into that hazy world of independent thought, where a man is not upheld by a crowd of other men's opinions, but where he must find a footing of his own. Among the mass of men, there is little or no resistance to conformity. Could the history of opinions be fully written, it would be seen how large a part in human proceedings the love of conformity, or rather the fear of non-conformity, has occasioned. It has triumphed over all other fears; over love, hate, pity, sloth, anger, truth, pride, comfort, self-interest, vanity, and maternal love. It has torn down the sense of beauty in the human soul, and set up in its place little ugly idols which it compels us to worship with more than Japanese devotion. It has contradicted Nature in the most obvious things, and been listened to with abject submission. Its empire has been no less extensive than deep-seated. The serf to custom points his finger at the slave to fashion—as if it signified whether it is an old or a new thing which is irrationally conformed to. The man of letters despises both the slaves of fashion and of custom, but often runs his narrow career of thought, shut up, though he sees it not, within close walls which he does not venture even to peep over.

It is hard to say in what department of human thought and endeavour conformity has triumphed most. Religion comes to one's mind first; and well it may when one thinks what men have conformed to in all ages in that matter. If we pass to art, or science, we shall see there too the wondrous slavery which men have endured—from puny fetters, moreover, which one stirring thought would, as we think, have burst asunder. The above, however, are matters not within every one's cognisance; some of them are shut in by learning or the show of it; and plain "practical" men would say, they follow where they have no business but to follow. But the way in which the human body shall be covered is not a thing for the scientific and the learned only: and is allowed on all hands to concern, in no small degree, one half at least of the creation. It is in such a simple thing as dress that each of us may form some estimate of the extent of conformity in the world. A wise nation, unsubdued by superstition, with the collected experience of peaceful ages, concludes that female feet are to be clothed by crushing them. The still wiser nations of the west have adopted a swifter mode of destroying health, and creating angularity, by crushing the upper part of the female body. In such matters nearly all people conform. Our brother man is seldom so bitter against us, as when we refuse to adopt at once his notions of the infinite. But even religious dissent were less dangerous and more respectable than dissent in dress. If you want to see what men will do in the way of conformity, take a European hat for your subject of meditation. I dare say there are twenty-two millions of people at this minute each wearing one of these hats in order to please the rest. As in the fine arts, and in architecture, especially, so in dress, something is often retained that was useful when something else was beside it. To go to architecture for an instance, a pinnacle is retained, not that it is of any use where it is, but in another kind of building it would have been. That style of building, as a whole, has gone out of fashion, but the pinnacle has somehow or other kept its ground and must be there, no one insolently going back to first principles and asking what is the use and object of building pinnacles. Similar instances in dress will occur to my readers. Some of us are not skilled in such affairs; but looking at old pictures we may sometimes see how modern clothes have attained their present pitch of frightfulness and inconvenience. This matter of dress is one in which, perhaps, you might expect the wise to conform to the foolish; and they have.

When we have once come to a right estimate of the strength of conformity, we shall, I think, be more kindly disposed to eccentricity than we usually are. Even a wilful or an absurd eccentricity is some support against the weighty common-place conformity of the world. If it were not for some singular people who persist in thinking for themselves, in seeing for themselves, and in being comfortable, we should all collapse into a hideous uniformity.

It is worth while to analyse that influence of the world which is the right arm of conformity. Some persons bend to the world in all things, from an innocent belief that what so many people think must be right. Others have a vague fear of the world as of some wild beast which may spring out upon them at any time. Tell them they are safe in their houses from this myriad-eyed creature: they still are sure that they shall meet with it some day, and would propitiate its favour at any sacrifice. Many men contract their idea of the world to their own circle, and what they imagine to be said in that circle of friends and acquaintances is their idea of public opinion—"as if," to use a saying of Southey's, "a number of worldlings made a world." With some unfortunate people, the much dreaded "world" shrinks into one person of more mental power than their own, or perhaps merely of coarser nature; and the fancy as to what this person will say about anything they do, sits upon them like a nightmare. Happy the man who can embark his small adventure of deeds and thoughts upon the shallow waters round his home, or send them afloat on the wide sea of humanity, with no great anxiety in either case as to what reception they may meet with! He would have them steer by the stars, and take what wind may come to them.

A reasonable watchfulness against conformity will not lead a man to spurn the aid of other men, still less to reject the accumulated mental capital of ages. It does not compel us to dote upon the advantages of savage life. We would not forego the hard-earned gains of civil society because there is something in most of them which tends to contract the natural powers, although it vastly aids them. We would not, for instance, return to the monosyllabic utterance of barbarous men, because in any formed language there are a thousand snares for the understanding. Yet we must be most watchful of them. And in all things, a man must beware of so conforming himself as to crush his nature and forego the purpose of his being. We must look to other standards than what men may say or think. We must not abjectly bow down before rules and usages; but must refer to principles and purposes. In few words, we must think, not whom we are following, but what we are doing. If not, why are we gifted with individual life at all? Uniformity does not consist with the higher forms of vitality. Even the leaves of the same tree are said to differ, each one from all the rest. And can it be good for the soul of a man " with a biography of his own like to no one else's," to subject itself without thought to the opinions and ways of others : not to grow into symmetry, but to be moulded down into conformity?

Ellesmere. Well, I rather like that essay. I was afraid, at first, it was going to have more of the fault into which you essay writers generally fall, of being a comment on the abuse of a thing, and not on the thing itself. There always seems to me to want another essay on the other side. But I think, at the end, you protect yourself against misconstruction. In the spirit of the essay, you know, of course, that I quite agree with you. Indeed, I differ from all the ordinary

biographers of that independent gentleman, Don't Care.
I believe Don't Care came to a good end.   At any rate
he came to some end.   Whereas numbers of people
never have beginning, or ending, of their own.   An
obscure dramatist, Milverton, whom we know of,
makes one of his characters say, in reply to some world-
fearing wretch:

> "While you, you think
> What others think, or what you think they'll say,
> Shaping your course by something scarce more tangible
> Than dreams, at best the shadows on the stream
> Of aspen leaves by flickering breezes swayed—
> Load me with irons, drive me from morn till night,
> I am not the utter slave which that man is
> Whose sole word, thought, and deed are built on what
> The world may say of him."

Milverton. Never mind the obscure dramatist. But,
Ellesmere, you really are unreasonable, if you suppose
that, in the limits of a short essay, you can accurately
distinguish all you write between the use and the abuse
of a thing.   The question is, will people misunderstand
you—not, is the language such as to be logically im-
pregnable?   Now, in the present case, no man will
really suppose it is a wise and just conformity that
I am inveighing against.

Ellesmere. I am not sure of that.   If everybody is
to have independent thought, would there not be a
fearful instability and want of compactness?   Another
thing, too—conformity often saves so much time and
trouble.

Milverton. Yes; it has its uses.   I do not mean, in

the world of opinion and morality, that it should be all elasticity and no gravitation; but at least enough elasticity to preserve natural form and independent being.

Ellesmere. I think it would have been better if you had turned the essay another way, and instead of making it on conformity, had made it ˉon interference. That is the greater mischief and the greater folly, I think. Why do people unreasonably conform? Because they feel unreasonable interference. War, I say, is interference on a small scale compared with the interference of private life. Then the absurdity on which it proceeds; that men are all alike, or that it is desirable that they should be; and that what is good for one is good for all.

Dunsford. I must say, I think, Milverton, you do not give enough credit for sympathy, good-nature, and humility as material elements in the conformity of the world.

Ellesmere. I am not afraid, my dear Dunsford, of the essay doing much harm. There is a power of sleepy conformity in the world. You may just startle your conformists for a minute, but they gravitate into their old way very soon. You talk of their humility, Dunsford, but I have heard people who have conformed to opinions, without a pretence of investigation, as arrogant and intolerant towards anybody who differed from them, as if they stood upon a pinnacle of independent sagacity and research.

Dunsford. One never knows, Ellesmere, on which side you are. I thought you were on mine a minute or two ago; and now you come down upon me with more than Milverton's anti-conforming spirit.

Ellesmere. The greatest mischief, as I take it, of this slavish conformity, is in the reticence it creates. People will be, what are called, intimate friends, and yet no real interchange of opinion takes place between them. A man keeps his doubts, his difficulties, and his peculiar opinions to himself. He is afraid of letting anybody know that he does not exactly agree with the world's theories on all points. There is no telling the hindrance that this is to truth.

Milverton. A great cause of this, Ellesmere, is in the little reliance you can have on any man's secrecy. A man finds that what, in the heat of discussion, and in the perfect carelessness of friendship, he has said to his friend, is quoted to people whom he would never have said it to; knowing that it would be sure to be misunderstood, or half-understood, by them. And so he grows cautious; and is very loth to communicate to anybody his more cherished opinions, unless they fall in exactly with the stream. Added to which, I think there is in these times less than there ever was of a proselytising spirit; and people are content to keep their opinions to themselves—more perhaps from indifference than from fear.

Ellesmere. Yes, I agree with you.

By the way, I think your taking dress as an illustration of extreme conformity is not bad. Really it is wonderful the degree of square and dull hideousness to which, in the process of time and tailoring, and by severe conformity, the human creature's outward appearance has arrived. Look at a crowd of men from a height, what an ugly set of ants they appear! Myself, when I see an Eastern man, one of the people attached᾽ to their embassies, sweeping by us in something flowing and stately, I feel inclined to take off my hat to him (only that I think the hat might frighten him), and say, Here is a great, unhatted, uncravated, bearded man, not a creature clipt and twisted and tortured into tailorhood.

Dunsford. Ellesmere broke in upon me just now, so that I did not say all that I meant to say. But, Milverton, what would you admit that we are to conform to? In silencing the general voice, may we not give too much opportunity to our own headstrong suggestions, and to wilful licence?

Milverton. Yes: to be somewhat deaf to the din of the world may be no gain, even loss, if then we only listen more to the worst part of ourselves; but in itself it is a good thing to silence that din. It is at least a beginning of good. If anything good is then gained, it is not a sheepish tendency, but an independent resolve growing out of our nature. And, after all, when we talk of non-conformity, it may only be that we non-conform to the immediate sect of thought or action about us, to conform to a much wider thing in human nature.

Ellesmere. Ah me! how one wants a moral essayist always at hand to enable one to make use of moral essays.

Milverton. Your rules of law are grand things—the proverbs of justice; yet has not each case its specialities, requiring to be argued with much circumstance, and capable of different interpretations? Words cannot be made into men.

Dunsford. I wonder you answer his sneers, Milverton.

Ellesmere. I must go and see whether words cannot be made into guineas: and then guineas into men is an easy thing. These trains will not wait even for critics, so, for the present, good-bye.

CHAPTER III.

ELLESMERE soon wrote us word that he would be able to come down again; and I agreed to be at Worth-Ashton (Milverton's house) on the day of his arrival. I had scarcely seated myself at our usual place of meeting before the friends entered, and after greeting me, the conversation thus began:

Ellesmere. Upon my word, you people who live in the country have a pleasant time of it. As Milverton was driving me from the station through Durley Wood, there was such a rich smell of pines, such a twittering of birds, so much joy, sunshine, and beauty, that I began to think, if there were no such place as London, it really would be very desirable to live in the country.

Milverton. What a climax! But I am always very suspicious, when Ellesmere appears to be carried away by any enthusiasm, that it will break off suddenly, like the gallop of a post-horse.

Dunsford. Well, what are we to have for our essay?

Milverton. Despair.

Ellesmere. I feel equal to anything just now, and so, if it must be read sometime or other, let us have it now.

Milverton. You need not be afraid. I want to take away, not to add gloom. Shall I read?

We assented, and he began.

DESPAIR.

Despair may be serviceable when it arises from a temporary prostration of spirits : during which the mind is insensibly healing, and her scattered power silently returning. This is better than to be the sport of a teasing hope without reason. But to indulge in despair as a habit is slothful, cowardly, short-sighted ; and manifestly tends against Nature. Despair is then the paralysis of the soul.

These are the principal causes of despair—remorse, the sorrows of the affections, worldly trouble, morbid views of religion, native melancholy.

REMORSE.

Remorse does but add to the evil which bred it, when it promotes, not penitence, but despair. To have erred in one branch of our duties does not unfit us for the performance of all the rest, unless we suffer the dark spot to spread over our whole nature, which may happen almost unobserved in the torpor of despair. This kind of despair is chiefly grounded on a foolish belief that individual words or actions constitute the whole life of man : whereas they are often not fair representatives of portions even of that life. The fragments of rock in a

mountain stream may tell much of its history. are in
fact results of its doings, but they are not the stream.
They were brought down when it was turbid ; it may
now be clear : they are as much the result of other
circumstances as of the action of the stream ; their
history is fitful : they give us no sure intelligence of
the future course of the stream, or of the nature of its
waters ; and may scarcely show more than that it has
not been always as it is. The actions of men are often
but little better indications of the men themselves.

A prolonged despair arising from remorse is unreasonable at any age, but if possible, still more so when
felt by the young. To think, for example, that the
great Being who made us could have made eternal ruin
and misery inevitable to a poor half-fledged creature of
eighteen or nineteen ! And yet how often has the pro-
foundest despair from remorse brooded over children of
that age and eaten into their hearts.

There is frequently much selfishness about remorse.
Put what has been done at the worst. Let a man see
his own evil word, or deed, in full light, and own it to
be black as hell itself. He is still here. He cannot be
isolated. There still remain for him cares and duties ;
and, therefore, hopes. Let him not in imagination link
all creation to his fate. Let him yet live in the welfare
of others, and, if it may be so, work out his own in this
way : if not, be content with theirs. The saddest cause
of remorseful despair is when a man does something
expressly contrary to his character : when an honourable
man, for instance, slides into some dishonourable action ;
or a tender-hearted man falls into cruelty from careless-

ness ; or, as often happens, a sensitive nature continues to give the greatest pain to others from temper, feeling all the time, perhaps, more deeply than the persons aggrieved. All these cases may be summed up in the words, "That which I would not that I do," the saddest of all human confessions, made by one of the greatest men. However, the evil cannot be mended by despair. Hope and humility are the only supports under this burden. As Mr. Carlyle says,

" What are faults, what are the outward details of a life; if the inner secret of it, the remorse, temptations, true, often-baffled, never-ended struggle of it, be forgotten. 'It is not in man that walketh to direct his steps.' Of all acts, is not, for a man, *repentance* the most divine ? The deadliest sin, I say, were that same supercilious consciousness of no sin ; that is death : the heart so conscious is divorced from sincerity, humility, and fact ; is dead : it is ' pure ' as dead dry sand is pure. David's life and history, as written for us in those Psalms of his, I consider to be the truest emblem ever given of a man's moral progress and warfare here below. All earnest souls will ever discern in it the faithful struggle of an earnest human soul towards what is good and best. Struggle often baffled, sore baffled, down as into entire wreck ; yet a struggle never ended ; ever, with tears, repentance, true unconquerable purpose, begun anew. Poor human nature ! is not a man's walking, in truth, always that : a ' succession of falls !' Man can do no other. In this wild element of a Life, he has to struggle onwards ; now fallen, deep abased ; and ever, with tears, repentance, with bleeding heart, he has to rise again, struggle again still onwards. That his struggle *be* a faithful unconquerable one : this is the question of questions."

THE SORROWS OF THE AFFECTIONS.

The loss by death of those we love has the first place
in these sorrows. Yet the feeling in this case, even
when carried to the highest, is not exactly despair,
having too much warmth in it for that. Not much can
be said in the way of comfort on this head. Queen
Elizabeth, in her hard, wise way, writing to a mother
who had lost her son, tells her that she will be com-
forted in time ; and why should she not do for herself
what the mere lapse of time will do for her ? Brave
words! and the stern woman, more earnest than the
sage in " Rasselas," would have tried their virtue on
herself. But I fear they fell somewhat coldly on the
mother's ear. Happily, in these bereavements, kind
Nature with her opiates, day by day administered, does
more than all the skill of the physician moralists. Sir
Thomas Browne says.

" Darkness and light divide the course of time, and
oblivion shares with memory a great part even of our living
beings ; we slightly remember our felicities, and the smartest
strokes of affliction leave but short smart upon us. Sense
endureth no extremities, and sorrows destroy us or themselves. To weep into stones are fables. Afflictions induce
callosities, miseries are slippery, or fall like snow upon us,
which, notwithstanding, is no unhappy stupidity. To be
ignorant of evils to come, and forgetful of evils past, is a
merciful provision in Nature, whereby we digest the mixture
of our few and evil days, and our delivered senses not re-
lapsing into cutting remembrances, our sorrows are not kept
raw by the edge of repetitions."

The good knight thus makes much comfort out of our physical weakness. But something may be done in a very different direction, namely, by spiritual strength. By elevating and purifying the sorrow, we may take it more out of matter, as it were, and so feel less the loss of what is material about it.

The other sorrows of the affections which may produce despair, are those in which the affections are wounded, as jealousy, love unrequited, friendship betrayed and the like. As, in despair from remorse, the whole life seems to be involved in one action : so in the despair we are now considering, the whole life appears to be shut up in the one unpropitious affection. Yet human nature, if fairly treated, is too large a thing to be suppressed into despair by one affection, however potent. We might imagine that if there were anything that would rob life of its strength and favour, it is domestic unhappiness. And yet how numerous is the bond of those whom we know to have been eminently unhappy in some domestic relation, but whose lives have been full of vigorous and kindly action. Indeed the culture of the world has been largely carried on by such men. As long as there is life in the plant, though it be sadly pent in, it will grow towards any opening of light that is left for it.

WORLDLY TROUBLE.

This appears too mean a subject for despair, or, at least, unworthy of having any remedy, or soothing thought out of it. Whether a man lives in a large room or a small one, rides or is obliged to walk, gets a plenteous

dinner every day, or a sparing one, do not seem matters
for despair. But the truth is, that worldly trouble, such,
for instance, as loss of fortune, is seldom the simple
thing that poets would persuade us.

> " The little or the much she gave is quietly resigned ;
> Content with poverty, my soul I arm,
> And virtue, though in rags will keep me warm."

So sings Dryden, paraphrasing Horace, but each of them,
with their knowledge of the world, cross-questioned in
prose, could have told us how the stings of fortune
really are felt. The truth is, that fortune is not exactly
a distinct isolated thing which can be taken away—
" and there an end." But much has to be severed,
with undoubted pain in the operation. A man mostly
feels that his reputation for sagacity, often his honour,
the comfort, too, or supposed comfort, of others are
embarked in his fortunes. Mere stoicism, and resolves
about fitting fortune to oneself, not oneself to
fortune, though good things enough in their way, will
not always meet the whole of the case. And a man
who could bear personal distress of any kind with
Spartan indifference, may suffer himself to be over-
whelmed by despair growing out of worldly trouble. A
frequent origin of such despair, as indeed of all despair
(not by any means excluding despair from remorse), is
pride. Let a man say to himself, " I am not the perfect
character I meant to be ; this is not the conduct I had
imagined for myself ; these are not the fortunate circumstances I had always intended to be surrounded by."
Let him at once admit that he is on a lower level than

his ideal one ; and then see what is to be done there. This seems the best way of treating all that part of worldly trouble which consists of self-reproval. We scarcely know of any outward life continuously prosperous (and a very dull one it would be): why should we expect the inner life to be one course of unbroken self-improvement, either in prudence, or in virtue ?

Before a man gives way to excessive grief about the fortunes of his family being lost with his own, he should think whether he really knows wherein lies the welfare of others. Give him some fairy power, inexhaustible purses or magic lamps, not, however, applying to the mind ; and see whether he could make those whom he would favour good or happy. In the East, they have a proverb of this kind, Happy are the children of those fathers who go to the Evil One. But for anything that our Western experience shows, the proverb might be reversed, and, instead of running thus, Happy are the sons of those who have got money anyhow, it might be. Happy are the sons of those who have failed in getting money. In fact, there is no sound proverb to be made about it either way. We know nothing about the matter. Our surest influence for good or evil over others is through themselves. Our ignorance of what is physically good for any man may surely prevent anything like despair with regard to that part of the fortunes of others dear to us, which, as we think, is bound up with our own.

MORBID VIEWS OF RELIGION.

As religion is the most engrossing subject that can be presented to us, it will be considered in all states of mind and by all minds. It is impossible but that the most hideous and perverted views of religion must arise. To combat the particular views which may be supposed to cause religious despair, would be too theological an undertaking for this essay. One thing only occurs to me to say, namely, that the lives and the mode of speaking about themselves adopted by the founders of Christianity, afford the best contradiction to religious melancholy that I believe can be met with.

NATIVE MELANCHOLY.

There is such a thing. Jacques, without the "sundry contemplation" of his travels, or any "simples" to "compound" his melancholy form, would have ever been wrapped in a "most humorous sadness." It was innate. This melancholy may lay its votaries open to any other cause of despair, but having mostly some touch of philosophy (if it be not absolutely morbid), it is not unlikely to preserve them from any extremity. It is not acute, but chronic.

It may be said in its favour that it tends to make men indifferent to their own fortunes. But then the sorrow of the world presses more deeply upon them. With large open hearts, the untowardness of things present, the miseries of the past, the mischief, stupidity, and error which reign in the world, at times almost crush your melancholy men. Still, out of their sadness may come their strength, or, at least, the best direction of it. Nothing, perhaps, is lost; not even sin—much less sorrow.

Ellesmere. I am glad you have ended as you have: for, previously, you seemed to make too much of getting rid of all distress of mind. I always liked that passage in " Philip van Artevelde," where Father John says,

" He that lacks time to mourn, lacks time to mend.
  Eternity mourns that."

You have a better memory than I have: how does it go on ?

Milverton.

  " 'Tis an ill cure
For life's worst ills, to have no time to feel them.
Where sorrow's held intrusive and turned out,
There wisdom will not enter, nor true power,
Nor aught that dignifies humanity."

Still this does not justify despair, which was what I was writing about.

Ellesmere. Perhaps it was not a just criticism of mine. One part of the subject you have certainly omitted. You do not tell us how much there often is of physical disorder in despair. I dare say you will think it a coarse and unromantic mode of looking at things; but I must confess I agree with what Leigh Hunt has said somewhere, that one can walk down distress of mind—even remorse, perhaps.

Milverton. Yes; I am for the Peripatetics against all other philosophers.

Ellesmere. By the way, there is a passage in one of Hazlitt's essays, I thought of while you were reading, about remorse and religious melancholy. He speaks of mixing up religion and morality; and then goes on to say, that Calvinistic notions have obscured and prevented self-knowledge. *

Give me the essay—there is a passage I want to look at. This comparison of life to a mountain stream, the rocks brought down by it being the actions, is too much worked out. When we speak of similes not going on four legs, it implies, I think, that a simile is at best but a four-legged animal. Now this is almost a centipede of a simile. I think I have had the same thought as yours here, and I have compared the life of an individual to a curve. You both smile. Now I

---

* The passage which must have been alluded to is this: "The stricter tenets of Calvinism, which allow no medium between grace and reprobation, and doom man to eternal punishment for every breach of the moral law, as an equal offence against Infinite truth and justice, proceed (like the paradoxical doctrine of the Stoics) from taking a half-view of this subject, and considering man as amenable only to the dictates of his understanding and his conscience, and not excusable from the temptations and frailty of human ignorance and passion. The mixing up of religion and morality together, or the making us accountable for every word, thought, or action, under no less a responsibility than our everlasting future welfare or misery, has also added incalculably to the difficulties of self-knowledge, has superinduced a violent and spurious state of feeling, and made it almost impossible to distinguish the boundaries between the true and false, in judging of human conduct and motives. A religious man is afraid of looking into the state of his soul, lest at the same time he should reveal it to heaven; and tries to persuade himself that by shutting his eyes to his true character and feelings, they will remain a profound secret, both here and hereafter."

thought that Dunsford at any rate would be pleased with this reminiscence of college days. But to proceed with my curve. You may have numbers of the points through which it passes given, and yet know nothing of the nature of the curve itself. See, now, it shall pass through here and here, but how it will go in the interval, what is the law of its being, we know not. But this simile would be too mathematical, I fear.

Milverton. I hold to the centipede.

Ellesmere. Not a word has Dunsford said all this time.

Dunsford. I like the essay. I was not criticising as we went along, but thinking that perhaps the greatest charm of books is, that we see in them that other men have suffered what we have. Some souls we ever find who could have responded to all our agony, be it what it may. This at least robs misery of its loneliness.

Ellesmere. On the other hand, the charm of intercourse with our fellows, when we are in sadness, is that they do not reflect it in any way. Each keeps his own trouble to himself, and often pretending to think and care about other things, comes to do so for the time.

Dunsford. Well, but you might choose books which would not reflect your troubles.

Ellesmere. But the fact of having to make a choice to do this, does away, perhaps, with some part of the benefit: whereas, in intercourse with living men, you take what you find, and you find that neither your trouble, nor any likeness of it, is absorbing other people. But this is not the whole reason: the truth is, the life and impulses of other men are catching; you cannot explain exactly how it is that they take you out of yourself.

Milverton. No man is so confidential as when he is addressing the whole world. You find, therefore, more comfort for sorrow in books than in social intercourse. I mean more direct comfort; for I agree with what Ellesmere says about society.

Ellesmere. In comparing men and books, one must always remember this important distinction—that one can put the books down at any time. As Macaulay says, "Plato is never sullen. Cervantes is never petulant. Demosthenes never comes unseasonably. Dante never stays too long."

Milverton. Besides, one can manage to agree so well, intellectually, with a book; and intellectual differences are the source of half the quarrels in the world.

Ellesmere. Judicious shelving!

Milverton. Judicious skipping will nearly do. Now when one's friend, or oneself, is crotchety, dogmatic, or disputatious, one cannot turn over to another day.

Ellesmere. Don't go, Dunsford. Here is a passage in the essay I meant to have said something about— "why should we expect the inner life to be one course of unbroken self-improvement," etc.—You recollect? Well, it puts me in mind of a conversation between a complacent poplar and a grim old oak, which I overheard the other day. The poplar said that it grew up quite straight, heavenwards, that all its branches pointed the same way, and always had done so.

Turning to the oak, which it had been talking at before for some time, the poplar went on to remark, that it did not wish to say anything unfriendly to a brother of the forest, but those warped and twisted branches seemed to show strange struggles. The tall thing concluded its oration by saying, that it grew up very fast, and that when it had done growing, it did not suffer itself to be made into huge floating engines of destruction. But different trees had different tastes. There was then a sound from the old oak, like an " ah " or a " whew," or, perhaps, it was only the wind amongst its resisting branches; and the gaunt creature said that it had had ugly winds from without and cross-grained impulses from within; that it knew it had thrown out awkwardly a branch here and a branch there, which would never come quite right again it feared; that men worked it up, sometimes for good and sometimes for evil—but that at any rate it had not lived for nothing. The poplar began again immediately, for this kind of tree can talk for ever, but I patted the old oak approvingly and went on.

Milverton. Well, your trees divide their discourse somewhat Ellesmerically : they do not talk with the simplicity La Fontaine's would; but there is a good deal in them. They are not altogether sappy.

Ellesmere. I really thought of this fable of mine the other day, as I was passing the poplar at the end of the valley, and I determined to give it you on the first occasion.

Dunsford. I hope, Ellesmere, you do not intend to put sarcastic notions into the sap of our trees hereabouts. There's enough of sarcasm in you to season a whole forest.

Ellesmere. Dunsford is afraid of what the trees may say to the country gentlemen, and whether they will be able to answer them. I will be careful not to make the trees too clever.

Milverton. Let us go and try if we can hear any more forest talk. The winds, shaped into voices by the leaves, say many things to us at all times.

CHAPTER IV.

IN the course of our walk Milverton promised to read the following essay on Recreation the next day. I have no note of anything that was said before the reading.

RECREATION.

This subject has not had the thought it merits. It seems trivial. It concerns some hours in the daily life of each of us; but it is not connected with any subject of human grandeur, and we are rather ashamed of it. Schiller has some wise, but hard words that relate to it. He perceives the pre-eminence of the Greeks, who could do many things. He finds that modern men are units of great nations; but not great units themselves. And there is some room for this reasoning of his.

Our modern system of division of labour divides wits also. The more necessity there is, therefore, for

finding in recreation something to expand men's intelligence. There are intellectual pursuits almost as
much divided as pin-making; and many a man goes
through some intellectual process, for the greater part
of his working hours, which corresponds with the
making of a pin's head. Must there not be some
danger of a general contraction of mind from this
convergence of attention upon something very small,
for so considerable a portion of a man's life?

What answer can civilisation give to this? It can
say that greater results are worked out by the modern
system; that though each man is doing less himself
than he might have done in former days, he sees
greater and better things accomplished; and that his
thoughts, not bound down by his petty occupation,
travel over the work of the human family. There is a
great deal, doubtless, in this argument; but man is
not altogether an intellectual recipient. He is a con-
structive animal also. It is not the knowledge that
you can pour into him that will satisfy him, or enable
him to work out his nature. He must see things for
himself: he must have bodily work and intellectual
work different from his bread-getting work; or he runs
the danger of becoming a contracted pedant with a
poor mind and a sickly body.

I have seen it quoted from Aristotle, that the end of
labour is to gain leisure. It is a great saying. We
have in modern times a totally wrong view of the
matter. Noble work is a noble thing, but not all work.
Most people seem to think that any business is in
itself something grand; that to be intensely employed,

for instance. about something which has no truth, beauty. or usefulness in it, which makes no man happier or wiser. is still the perfection of human endeavour, so that the work be intense. It is the intensity, not the nature. of the work that men praise. You see the extent of this feeling in little things. People are so ashamed of being caught for a moment idle, that if you come upon the most industrious servants or workmen whilst they are standing looking at something which interests them, or fairly resting, they move off in a fright. as if they were proved, by a moment's relaxation, to be neglectful of their work. Yet it is the result that they should mainly be judged by, and to which they should appeal. But amongst all classes, the working itself. incessant working, is the thing deified. Now what is the end and object of most work? To provide for animal wants. Not a contemptible thing by any means. but still it is not all in all with man. Moreover. in those cases where the pressure of bread-getting is fairly past, we do not often find men's exertions lessened on that account. There enter into their minds as motives, ambition, a love of hoarding, or a fear of leisure—things which, in moderation, may be defended or even justified; but which are not so peremptory, and upon the face of them excellent, that they at once dignify excessive labour.

The truth is, that to work insatiably requires much less mind than to work judiciously, and less courage than to refuse work that cannot be done honestly. For a hundred men whose appetite for work can be driven on by vanity. avarice, ambition, or a mistaken notion of advancing their families, there is about one who is desirous of expanding his own nature and the nature of others in all directions, of cultivating many pursuits, of bringing himself and those around him in contact with the universe in many points, of being a man and not a machine.

It may seem as if the preceding arguments were directed rather against excessive work than in favour of recreation. But the first object in an essay of this kind should be to bring down the absurd estimate that is often formed of mere work. What ritual is to the formalist, or contemplation to the devotee, business is to the man of the world. He thinks he cannot be doing wrong as long as he is doing that.

No doubt hard work is a great police agent. If everybody were worked from morning till night and then carefully locked up, the register of crimes might be greatly diminished. But what would become of human nature? Where would be the room for growth in such a system of things? It is through sorrow and mirth, plenty and need, a variety of passions, circumstances, and temptations, even through sin and misery, that men's natures are developed.

Again, there are people who would say, "Labour is not all; we do not object to the cessation of labour—a mere provision for bodily ends; but we fear the lightness and vanity of what you call recreation." Do these people take heed of the swiftness of thought—of the impatience of thought? What will the great mass of men be thinking of, if they are taught to shun amusements and the thoughts of amusement? If any sensuality is left open to them, they will think of that. If not sensuality, then avarice, or ferocity for "the cause of God," as they would call it. People who have had nothing else to amuse them have been very apt to indulge themselves in the excitement of persecuting their fellow creatures.

Our nation, the northern part of it especially, is given to believe in the sovereign efficacy of dulness. To be sure, dulness and solid vice are apt to go hand in hand. But then, according to our notions, dulness is in itself so good a thing—almost a religion.

Now, if ever a people required to be amused, it is we sad-hearted Anglo-Saxons. Heavy eaters, hard thinkers, often given up to a peculiar melancholy of our own, with a climate that for months together would frown away mirth if it could—many of us with very gloomy thoughts about our hereafter—if ever there were a people who should avoid increasing their dulness by all work and no play, we are that people. "They took their pleasure sadly," says Froissart, "after their fashion." We need not ask of what nation Froissart was speaking.

There is a theory which has done singular mischief to the cause of recreation and of general cultivation. It is that men cannot excel in more things than one; and that if they can, they had better be quiet about it. "Avoid music, do not cultivate art, be not known to excel in any craft but your own," says many a worldly parent, thereby laying the foundation of a narrow, greedy character, and destroying means of happiness and of improvement which success, or even real excellence, in one profession only cannot give. This is, indeed, a sacrifice of the end of living for the means.

Another check to recreation is the narrow way in which people have hitherto been brought up at schools and colleges. The classics are pre-eminent works. To acquire an accurate knowledge of them is an admirable discipline. Still, it would be well to give a youth but few of these great works, and so leave time for various arts, accomplishments, and knowledge of external things exemplified by other means than books. If this cannot be done but by over-working, then it had better not be done; for of all things, that must be avoided. But surely it can be done. At present, many a man who is versed in Greek metre, and afterwards full of law reports, is childishly ignorant of Nature. Let him walk with an intelligent child for a morning, and the child will ask him a hundred questions about sun, moon, stars, plants, birds, building, farming, and the like, to which he can give very sorry answers, if any; or, at the best, he has but a secondhand acquaintance with Nature. Men's conceits are his main knowledge. Whereas, if he had any pursuits connected with Nature, all Nature is in harmony with it, is brought into his presence by it, and it affords at once cultivation and recreation.

But, independently of those cultivated pursuits which form a high order of recreation, boyhood should never pass without the boy's learning several modes of recreation of the humbler kind. A parent or teacher seldom does a kinder thing by the child under his care than when he instructs it in some manly exercise, some pursuit connected with Nature out of doors, or even some domestic game. In hours of fatigue, anxiety, sickness, or worldly ferment, such means of amusement may delight the grown-up man when other things would fail.

An indirect advantage, but a very considerable one, attendant upon various modes of recreation, is, that they provide opportunities of excelling in something to boys and men who are dull in things which form the staple of education. A boy cannot see much difference between the nominative and the genitive cases—still less any occasion for aorists—but he is a good hand at some game or other; and he keeps up his self-respect, and the respect of others for him, upon his prowess in that game. He is better and happier on that account. And it is well, too, that the little world around him should know that excellence is not all of one form.

There are no details about recreation in this essay, the object here being mainly to show the worth of re-creation, and to defend it against objections from the over-busy and the over-strict. The sense of the beautiful, the desire for comprehending Nature, the love of personal skill and prowess, are not things implanted in men merely to be absorbed in producing and distributing the objects of our most obvious animal wants. If civilisation required this, civilisation would be a failure. Still less should we fancy that we are serving the cause of godliness when we are dis-couraging recreation. Let us be hearty in our pleasures, as in our work, and not think that the gracious Being

Who has made us so open-hearted to delight, looks with dissatisfaction at our enjoyment, as a hard task-master might, who in the glee of his slaves could see only a hindrance to their profitable working. And with reference to our individual cultivation, we may remember that we are not here to promote incalculable quantities of law, physic, or manufactured goods, but to become men—not narrow pedants, but wide-seeing, mind-travelled men. Who are the men of history to be admired most? Those whom most things became—who could be weighty in debate, of much device in council, considerate in a sick-room, genial at a feast, joyous at a festival, capable of discourse with many minds, large-souled, not to be shrivelled up into any one form, fashion, or temperament. Their contemporaries would have told us that men might have various accomplishments and hearty enjoyments, and not for that be the less effective in business, or less active in benevolence. I distrust the wisdom of asceticism as much as I do that of sensuality; Simeon Stylites no less than Sardanapalus.

Ellesmere. You alluded to Schiller at the beginning of the essay: can you show me his own words? I have a lawyer's liking for the best evidence.

Milverton. When we go in, I will show you some passages which bear me out in what I have made him say—at least, if the translation is faithful.*

* This was one of the passages which Milverton afterwards read to us:—

"Thus, however much may be gained for the world as a

Ellesmere. I have had a great respect for Schiller ever since I heard that saying of his about death, " Death cannot be an evil, for it is universal."

Dunsford. Very noble and full of faith.

Ellesmere. Touching the essay, I like it well enough ; but, perhaps, people will expect to find more about recreation itself—not only about the good of it, but what it is, and how it is to be got.

Milverton. I do not incline to go into detail about the matter. The object was to say something for the

whole by this fragmentary cultivation, it is not to be denied that the individuals whom it befalls are cursed for the benefit of the world. An athletic frame, it is true, is fashioned by gymnastic exercises ; but a form of beauty only by free and uniform action. Just so the exertions of single talents can create extraordinary men indeed ; but happy and perfect men only by their uniform temperature. And in what relation should we stand, then, to the past and coming ages, if the cultivation of human nature made necessary such a sacrifice ? We should have been the slaves of humanity, and drudged for her century after century, and stamped upon our mutilated natures the humiliating traces of our bondage—that the coming race might nurse its moral healthfulness in blissful leisure, and unfold the free growth of its humanity !

" But can it be intended that man should neglect himself for any particular design ? Ought Nature to deprive us, by its design, of a perfection which Reason, by its own, prescribes to us ? Then it must be false that the development of single faculties makes the sacrifice of totality necessary ; or, if indeed the law of Nature presses thus heavily, it becomes us to restore, by a higher art, this totality in our nature which art has destroyed."—*The Philosophical and Æsthetical Letters and Essays of* SCHILLER, *Translated by* J. WEISS, pp. 74, 75.

respectability of recreation, not to write a chapter of a book of sports. People must find out their own ways of amusing themselves.

Ellesmere. I will tell you what is the paramount thing to be attended to in all amusements—that they should be short. Moralists are always talking about " short-lived" pleasures : would that they were !

Dunsford. Hesiod told the world, some two thousand years ago, how much greater the half is than the whole.

Ellesmere. Dinner-givers and managers of theatres should forthwith be made aware of that fact. What a sacrifice of good things, and of the patience and comfort of human beings, a cumbrous modern dinner is ! I always long to get up and walk about.

Dunsford. Do not talk of modern dinners. Think what a Roman dinner must have been.

Milverton. Very true. It has always struck me that there is something quite military in the sensualism of the Romans—an " arbiter bibendi" chosen, and the whole feast moving on with fearful precision and apparatus of all kinds. Come, come! the world's improving, Ellesmere.

Ellesmere. Had the Romans public dinners ? Answer me that. Imagine a Roman, whose theory, at least, of a dinner was that it was a thing for enjoyment, whereas we often look on it as a continuation of the business of the day—I say, imagine a Roman girding himself up, literally girding himself up to make an after-dinner speech.

Milverton. I must allow that is rather a barbarous practice.

Ellesmere. If charity, or politics, cannot be done without such things, I suppose they are useful in their way; but let nobody ever imagine that they are **a form** of pleasure. People smearing each other over with stupid flattery, and most of the company being in dread of receiving some compliment which should oblige them to speak!

Dunsford. I should have thought, now, that you would always have had something to say, and therefore that you would not be so bitter against after-dinner speaking.

Ellesmere. No; when I have nothing to say, I can say nothing.

Milverton. Would it not be a pleasant thing if rich people would ask their friends sometimes to public amusements—order a play for them, for instance—or at any rate, provide some manifest amusement? They might, occasionally with great advantage, abridge the expense of their dinners, and throw it into other channels of hospitality.

Ellesmere. Ah, if they would have good acting at their houses, that would be very delightful; but I cannot say that the being taken to any place of public amusement would much delight me. By the way, Milverton, what do you say of theatres in the way of recreation? This decline of the drama, too, is a thing you must have thought about: let us hear your notions.

Milverton. I think one of the causes sometimes assigned, that reading is more spread, is a true and an important one; but, otherwise, I fancy that the present decline of the drama depends upon very small things which might be remedied. As to a love of the drama going out of the human heart, that is all nonsense. Put it at the lowest, what a great pleasure it is to hear a good play read. And again, as to serious pursuits unfitting men for dramatic entertainments, it is quite the contrary. A man, wearied with care and business, would find more change of ideas with less fatigue, in seeing a good play, than in almost any other way of amusing himself.

Dunsford. What are the causes then of the decline of the drama ?

Milverton. In England, or rather in London,—for London is England for dramatic purposes ; in London, then, theatrical arrangements seem to be framed to drive away people of sense. The noisome atmosphere, the difficult approach, the over-size of the great theatres, the intolerable length of performances.

Ellesmere. Hear ! hear !

Milverton. The crowding together of theatres in one part of the town, the lateness of the hours——

Ellesmere. The folly of the audience, who always applaud in the wrong place——

Dunsford. There is no occasion to say any more; I am quite convinced.

Milverton. But these annoyances need not be. Build a theatre of moderate dimensions ; give it great facility of approach ; take care that the performances never exceed three hours ; let lions and dwarfs pass by without any endeavour to get them within the walls ; lay aside all ambition of making stage waves which may almost equal real Ramsgate waves to our cockney apprehensions.   Of course there must be good players and good plays.

Ellesmere. Now we come to the part of Hamlet.

Milverton. Good players and good plays are both to be had if there were good demand for them.   But, I was going to say, let there be all these things, especially let there be complete ventilation, and the theatre will have the most abundant success.   Why, that one thing alone, the villainous atmosphere at most public places, is enough to daunt any sensible man from going to them.

Dunsford. There should be such a choice of plays—not merely Chamberlain-clipt—as any man or woman could go to.

Milverton. There should be certainly, but how is such a choice to be made, if the people who could regulate it, for the most part, stay away?   It is a dangerous thing, the better classes leaving any great source of amusement and instruction wholly, or greatly, to the less refined classes.

Dunsford. Yes, I must confess it is.

Great part of your arguments apply to musical as well as to theatrical entertainments.   Do you find similar results with respect to them?

Milverton. Why, they are not attended by any means as they would be, or made what they might be, if the objections I mentioned were removed.

Dunsford. What do you say to the out-of-door entertainments for a town population?

Milverton. As I said before, my dear Dunsford, I cannot give you a chapter of a "Book of Sports."

There ought, of course, to be parks for all quarters of the town: and I confess it would please me better to see, in holiday times and hours of leisure, hearty games going on in these parks, than a number of people sauntering about in uncomfortably new and unaccustomed clothes.

Ellesmere. Do you not see, Dunsford, that, like a cautious official man, he does not want to enter into small details, which have always an air of ridicule? He is not prepared to pledge himself to cricket, golf, football, or prisoner's bars; but in his heart he is manifestly a Young Englander—without the white waistcoat. Nothing would please him better than to see in large letters, on one of those advertising vans, "Great match! Victoria Park!! Eleven of Fleet Street against the Eleven of Saffron Hill!!!"

Milverton. Well, there is a great deal in the spirit of Young England that I like very much, indeed that I respect.

Ellesmere. I should like the Young England party better myself if I were quite sure there was no connection between them and a clan of sour, pity-mongering people, who wash one away with eternal talk about the contrast between riches and poverty; with whom a poor man is always virtuous; and who would, if they could, make him as envious and as discontented as possible.

Milverton. Nothing can be more strikingly in contrast with such thinkers than Young England. Young Englanders, according to the best of their theories, ought to be men of warm sympathy with all classes.

There is no doubt of this, that very seldom does any good thing arise, but there comes an ugly phantom of a caricature of it, which sidles up against the reality, mouths its favourite words as a third-rate actor does a great part, under-mimics its wisdom, over-acts its folly, is by half the world taken for it, goes some way to suppress it in its own time, and, perhaps, lives for it in history.

Ellesmere. Well brought out, that metaphor, but I don't know that it means more than that the followers of a system do in general a good deal to corrupt it, or that when a great principle is worked into human affairs, a considerable accretion of human folly and falseness mostly grows round it : which things some of us had a suspicion of before.

Dunsford. To go back to the subject. What would you do for country amusements, Milverton ? That is what concerns me, you know.

Milverton. Athletic amusements go on naturally here : do not require so much fostering as in towns. The commons must be carefully kept : I have quite a Cobbettian fear of their being taken away from us under some plausible pretext or other. Well, then, it strikes me that a great deal might be done to promote the more refined pleasures of life among our rural population. I hope we shall live to see many of Hullah's pupils playing an important part in this way. Of course, the foundation for these things may best be laid at schools ; and is being laid in some places, I am happy to say.

Ellesmere. Humph, music, sing-song !

Milverton. Don't you observe, Dunsford, that when Ellesmere wants to attack us, and does not exactly see how, he mutters to himself sarcastically, sneering himself up, as it were, to the attack.

Ellesmere. You and Dunsford are both wild for music, from barrel-organs upwards.

Milverton. I confess to liking the humblest attempts at melody.

Dunsford. I feel as Sir Thomas Browne tells us he felt, that " even that vulgar and tavern music, which makes one man merry, another mad, strikes in me a deep fit of devotion and a profound contemplation of the first composer. There is something in it of divinity more than the ear discovers; it is an hieroglyphical and shadowed lesson of the whole world and creatures of God : such a melody to the ear as the whole world well understood, would afford the understanding."

Milverton. Apropos of music in country places, when I was going about last year in the neighbouring county, I saw such a pretty scene at one of the towns. They had got up a band, which played once a week in the evening. It was a beautiful summer evening, and the window of my room at the end overlooked the open space they had chosen for their performances. There was the great man of the neighbourhood in his carriage looking as if he came partly on duty, as well as for pleasure. Then there were burly tradesmen, with an air of quiet satisfaction, sauntering about, or leaning against railings. Some were no doubt critical—thought that Will Miller did not play as well as usual this evening. Will's young wife, who had come out to look again at him in his band dress (for the band had a uniform), thought differently. Little boys broke out into imaginary polkas, having some distant reference to the music: not without grace though. The sweep was pre-eminent: as if he would say, "Dirty and sooty as I am I have a great deal of fun in me. Indeed, what would May-day be but for me?" Studious little boys of the free-school, all green grasshopper-looking, walked about as boys knowing something of Latin. Here and there went a couple of them in childish loving way, with their arms about each other's necks. Matrons and shy young maidens sat upon the door-steps near. Many a merry laugh filled up the interludes of music. And when evening came softly down upon us, the band finished with " God save the Queen," the little circle of those who would hear the last note moved off, there was a clattering of shutters, a shining of lights through casement-windows, and soon the only sound to be heard was the rough voice of some villager, who would have been too timid to adventure anything by daylight, but now sang boldly out as he went homewards.

Ellesmere. Very pretty, but it sounds to me somewhat fabulous.

Milverton. I assure you——

Ellesmere. Yes, you were tired, had a good dinner, read a speech for or against the corn-laws, fell asleep of course, and had this ingenious dream, which, to this day, you believe to have been a reality. I understand it all.

Milverton. I wish I could have many more such dreams.

CHAPTER V.

OUR last conversation broke off abruptly on the entrance of a visitor: we forgot to name a time for our next meeting; and when I came again, I found Milverton alone in his study. He was reading Count Rumford's essays.

Dunsford. So you are reading Count Rumford. What is it that interests you there?

Milverton. Everything he writes about. He is to me a delightful writer. He throws so much life into all his writings. Whether they are about making the most of food or fuel, or propounding the benefits of bathing, or inveighing against smoke, it is that he went and saw and did and experimented himself upon himself. His proceedings at Munich to feed the poor are more interesting than many a novel. It is surprising, too, how far he was before the world in all the things he gave his mind to.

Here Ellesmere entered.

Ellesmere. I heard you were come, Dunsford: I hope we shall have an essay to-day. My critical faculties have been dormant for some days, and want to be roused a little. Milverton was talking to you about Count Rumford when I came in, was he not? Ah, the Count is a great favourite with Milverton when he is down here; but there is a book upstairs which is Milverton's real favourite just now, a portentous-looking book; some relation to a blue-book.

something about sewerage, or health of towns, or public improvements, over which said book our friend here goes into enthusiasms. I am sure if it could be reduced to the size of that tatterdemalion Horace that he carries about, the poor little Horace would be quite supplanted.

Milverton. Now, I must tell you, Dunsford, that Ellesmere himself took up this book he talks about, and it was a long time before he put it down.

Ellesmere. Yes, there is something in real life, even though it is in the unheroic part of it, that interests one. I mean to get through the book.

Dunsford. What are we to have to-day for our essay?

Milverton. Let us adjourn to the garden, and I will read you an essay on Greatness, if I can find it.

We went to our favourite place, and Milverton read us the following essay.

GREATNESS.

You cannot substitute any epithet for great, when you are talking of great men. Greatness is not general dexterity carried to any extent; nor proficiency in any one subject of human endeavour. There are great astronomers, great scholars, great painters, even great poets who are very far from great men. Greatness can do without success and with it. William is greater in his retreats than Marlborough in his victories. On the other hand, the uniformity of Cæsar's success does not dull his greatness. Greatness is not in the circumstances, but in the man.

What does this greatness then consist in ? Not in a nice balance of qualities, purposes, and powers. That will make a man happy, a successful man, a man always in his right depth. Nor does it consist in absence of errors. We need only glance back at any list that can be made of great men, to be convinced of that. Neither does greatness consist in energy, though often accompanied by it. Indeed, it is rather the breadth of the waters than the force of the current that we look to, to fulfil our idea of greatness. There is no doubt that energy acting upon a nature endowed with the qualities that we sum up in the word cleverness, and directed to a few clear purposes, produces a great effect, and may sometimes be mistaken for greatness. If a man is mainly bent upon his own advancement, it cuts many a difficult knot of policy for him, and gives a force and distinctness to his mode of going on which looks grand. The same happens if he has one pre-eminent idea of any kind, even though it should be a narrow one. Indeed, success in life is mostly gained by unity of purpose ; whereas greatness often fails by reason of its having manifold purposes, but it does not cease to be greatness on that account.

If greatness can be shut up in qualities, it will be found to consist in courage and in openness of mind and soul. These qualities may not seem at first to be so potent. But see what growth there is in them. The education of a man of open mind is never ended. Then, with openness of soul, a man sees some way into all other souls that come near him, feels with them, has their experience, is in himself a people. Sympathy

c—212

is the universal solvent. Nothing is understood without it. The capacity of a man, at least for understanding, may almost be said to vary according to his powers of sympathy. Again, what is there that can counteract selfishness like sympathy? Selfishness may be hedged in by minute watchfulness and self-denial, but it is counteracted by the nature being encouraged to grow out and fix its tendrils upon foreign objects.

The immense defect that want of sympathy is, may be strikingly seen in the failure of the many attempts that have been made in all ages to construct the Christian character, omitting sympathy. It has produced numbers of people walking up and down one narrow plank of self-restraint, pondering over their own merits and demerits, keeping out, not the world exactly, but their fellow-creatures from their hearts, and caring only to drive their neighbours before them on this plank of theirs, or to push them headlong. Thus, with many virtues, and much hard work at the formation of character, we have had splendid bigots or censorious small people.

But sympathy is warmth and light too. It is, as it were, the moral atmosphere connecting all animated natures. Putting aside, for a moment, the large differences that opinions, language, and education make between men, look at the innate diversity of character. Natural philosophers were amazed when they thought they had found a new-created species. But what is each man but a creature such as the world has not before seen? Then think how they pour forth in multitudinous masses, from princes delicately nurtured to little boys on scrubby commons, or in dark cellars. How are these people to be understood, to be taught to understand each other, but by those who have the deepest sympathies with all ?   There cannot be a great man without large sympathy.   There may be men who play loud-sounding parts in life without it, as on the stage, where kings and great people sometimes enter who are only characters of secondary import--deputy great men.   But the interest and the instruction lie with those who have to feel and suffer most.

Add courage to this openness we have been considering, and you have a man who can own himself in the wrong, can forgive, can trust, can adventure, can, in short, use all the means that insight and sympathy endow him with.

I see no other essential characteristics in the greatness of nations than there are in the greatness of individuals. Extraneous circumstances largely influence nations as individuals ; and make a larger part of the show of the former than of the latter ; as we are wont to consider no nation great that is not great in extent or resources, as well as in character. But of two nations, equal in other respects, the superiority must belong to the one which excels in courage and openness of mind and soul.

Again, in estimating the relative merits of different periods of the world, we must employ the same tests of greatness that we use to individuals. To compare, for instance, the present and the past. What astounds us

most in the past is the wonderful intolerance and
cruelty: a cruelty constantly turning upon the inventors:
an intolerance provoking ruin to the thing it would
foster. The most admirable precepts are thrown from
time to time upon this cauldron of human affairs, and
oftentimes they only seem to make it blaze the higher.
We find men devoting the best part of their intellects
to the invariable annoyance and persecution of their
fellows. You might think that the earth brought forth
with more abundant fruitfulness in the past than now,
seeing that men found so much time for cruelty, but
that you read of famines and privations which these
latter days cannot equal. The recorded violent deaths
amount to millions. And this is but a small part of the
matter. Consider the modes of justice; the use of
torture, for instance. What must have been the blinded
state of the wise persons (wise for their day) who used
torture? Did they ever think themselves, "What should
we not say if we were subjected to this?" Many times
they must really have desired to get at the truth; and
such was their mode of doing it. Now, at the risk of
being thought "a laudator" of time present, I would
say, here is the element of greatness we have made
progress in. We are more open in mind and soul. We
have arrived (some of us at least) at the conclusion that
men may honestly differ without offence. We have
learned to pity each other more. There is a greatness
in modern toleration which our ancestors knew not.

Then comes the other element of greatness, courage.
Have we made progress in that? This is a much more
dubious question. The subjects of terror vary so much

in different times that it is difficult to estimate the different degrees of courage shown in resisting them. Men fear public opinion now as they did in former times the Star Chamber; and those awful goddesses, Appearances, are to us what the Fates were to the Greeks. It is hardly possible to measure the courage of a modern against that of an ancient; but I am unwilling to believe but that enlightenment must strengthen courage.

The application of the tests of greatness, as in the above instance, is a matter of detail and of nice appreciation, as to the results of which men must be expected to differ largely: the tests themselves remain invariable —openness of nature to admit the light of love and reason, and courage to pursue it.

Ellesmere. I agree to your theory, as far as openness of nature is concerned; but I do not much like to put that half-brute thing, courage, so high.

Milverton. Well, you cannot have greatness without it: you may have well-intentioned people and far-seeing people; but if they have no stoutness of heart, they will only be shifty or remonstrant, nothing like great.

Ellesmere. You mean will, not courage. Without will, your open-minded, open-hearted man may be like a great, rudderless vessel driven about by all winds: not a small craft, but a most uncertain one.

Milverton. No, I mean both: both will and courage. Courage is the body to will.

Ellesmere. I believe you are right in that; but do not omit will. It amused me to see how you brought in one of your old notions—that this age is not contemptible. You scribbling people are generally on the other side.

Milverton. You malign us. If I must give any account for my personal predilection for modern times, it consists perhaps in this, that we may now speak our mind. What Tennyson says of his own land,

> " The land where, girt with friend or foe,
> A man may say the thing he will,"—

may be said, in some measure, of the age in which we live. This is an inexpressible comfort. This doubles life. These things surely may be said in favour of the present age, not with a view to puff it up, but so far to encourage ourselves, as we may by seeing that the world does not go on for nothing, that all the misery, blood, and toil that have been spent, were not poured out in vain. Could we have our ancestors again before us, would they not rejoice at seeing what they had purchased for us : would they think it any compliment to them to extol their times at the expense of the present, and so to intimate that their efforts had led to nothing ?

Ellesmere. "I doubt," as Lord Eldon would have said ; no, upon second thoughts, I do not doubt. I feel assured that a good many of these said ancestors you are calling up would be much discomforted at finding that all their suffering had led to no sure basis of persecution of the other side.

Dunsford. I wonder, Ellesmere, what you would have done in persecuting times. What escape would your sarcasm have found for itself ?

Milverton. Some orthodox way, I daresay. I do not

think he would have been particularly fond of martyrdom.

Ellesmere. No. I have no taste for making torches for truth, or being one : I prefer humane darkness to such illumination. At the same time one cannot tell lies ; and if one had been questioned about the incomprehensibilities which men in former days were so fierce upon, one must have shown that one disagreed with all parties.

Dunsford. Do not say "one :" *I* should not have disagreed with the great Protestant leaders in the Reformation, for instance.

Ellesmere. Humph.

Milverton. If we get aground upon the Reformation, we shall never push off again—else would I say something far from complimentary to those Protestant proceedings which we may rather hope were Tudoresque than Protestant.

Ellesmere. No, that is not fair. The Tudors were a coarse, fierce race ; but it will not do to lay the faults of their times upon them only. Look at Elizabeth's ministers. They had about as much notion of religious tolerance as they had of Professor Wheatstone's telegraph. It was not a growth of that age.

Milverton. I do not know. You have Cardinal Pole and the Earl of Essex, both tolerant men in the midst of bigots.

Ellesmere. Well, as you said, Milverton, we shall never push off, if we once get aground on this subject.

Dunsford. I am in fault : so I will take upon myself to bring you quite away from the Reformation. I have been thinking of that comparison in the essay of the present with the past. Such comparisons seem to me very useful, as they best enable us to understand our own times. And, then, when we have ascertained the state and tendency of our own age, we ought to strive to enrich it with those qualities which are complementary to its own. Now with all this toleration, which delights you so much, dear Milverton, is it not an age rather deficient in caring about great matters?

Milverton. If you mean great speculative matters, I might agree with you; but if you mean what I should call the greatest matters, such as charity, humanity, and the like, I should venture to differ with you, Dunsford.

Dunsford. I do not like to see the world indifferent to great speculative matters. I then fear shallowness and earthiness.

Milverton. It is very difficult to say what the world is thinking of now. It is certainly wrong to suppose that this is a shallow age because it is not driven by one impulse. As civilisation advances, it becomes more difficult to estimate what is going on, and we set it all down as confusion. Now there is not one " great antique heart," whose beatings we can count, but many impulses, many circles of thought in which men are moving many objects. Men are not all in the same state of progress, so cannot be moved in masses as of old. At one time chivalry urged all men, then the Church, and the phenomena were few, simple, and broad, or at least they seem so in history.

Ellesmere. Very true; still I agree somewhat with

Dunsford, that men are not agitated as they used to be by the great speculative questions. I account for it in this way, that the material world has opened out before us, and we cannot but look at that, and must play with it and work at it. I would say, too, that philosophy had been found out, and there is something in that. Still, I think if it were not for the interest now attaching to material things, great intellectual questions, not exactly of the old kind, would arise and agitate the world.

Milverton. There is one thing in my mind that may confirm your view. I cannot but think that the enlarged view we have of the universe must in some measure damp personal ambition. What is it to be a King, Sheik, Tetrarch, or Emperor, over a bit of a little bit? Macbeth's speech, " we'd jump the life to come," is a thing a man with modern lights, however madly ambitious, would hardly utter.

Dunsford. Religious lights, Milverton.

Milverton. Of course not, if he had them; but I meant scientific lights. Sway over our fellow-creatures, at any rate anything but mental sway, has shrunk into less proportions.

Ellesmere. I have been looking over the essay. I think you may put in somewhere—that that age would probably be the greatest in which there was the least difference between great men and the people in general —when the former were only neglected, not hunted down.

Milverton. Yes.

Ellesmere. You are rather lengthy here about the

cruelties to be found in history; but we are apt to forget these matters.

Milverton. They always press upon my mind.

Dunsford. And on mine. I do not like to read much of history for that very reason. I get so sick at heart about it all.

Milverton. Ah, yes, history is a stupendous thing. To read it is like looking at the stars; we turn away in awe and perplexity. Yet there is some method running through the little affairs of man as through the multitude of suns, seemingly to us as confused as routed armies in full flight.

Dunsford. Some law of love.

Ellesmere. I am afraid it is not in the past alone that we should be awe-struck with horrors: we, who have a slave-trade still on earth. But, to go back to the essay, I like what you say about the theory of constructing the Christian character without geniality; only you do not go far enough. You are afraid. People are for ever talking, especially you philanthropical people, about making others happy. I do not know any way so sure of making others happy as of being so oneself, to begin with. I do not mean that people are to be self-absorbed; but they are to drink in nature and life a little. From a genial, wisely-developed man good things radiate; whereas you must allow, Milverton, that benevolent people are very apt to be one-sided and fussy, and not of the sweetest temper if others will not be good and happy in their way.

Milverton. That is really not fair. Of course, acid, small-minded people carry their narrow notions and their acidity into their benevolence. Benevolence is no abstract perfection. Men will express their benevolence according to their other gifts or want of gifts. If it is strong, it overcomes other things in the character which would be hindrances to it ; but it must speak in the language of the soul it is in.

Ellesmere. Come, let us go and see the pigs. I hear them grunting over their dinners in the farmyard. I like to see creatures who can be happy without a theory.

CHAPTER VI.

THE next time that I came over to Worth-Ashton it was raining, and I found my friends in the study.

" Well, Dunsford," said Ellesmere, " is it not comfortable to have our sessions here for once, and to be looking out on a good solid English wet day ? "

Dunsford. Rather a fluid than a solid. But I agree with you in thinking it is very comfortable here.

Ellesmere. I like to look upon the backs of books. First I think how much of the owner's inner life and character is shown in his books ; then perhaps I wonder how he got such a book which seems so remote from all that I know of him——

Milverton. I shall turn my books the wrong side upwards when you come into the study.

Ellesmere. But what amuses me most is to see the odd way in which books get together, especially in the library of a man who reads his books and puts them up again wherever there is room. Now here is a charming party : "A Treatise on the Steam-Engine" between "Locke on Christianity" and Madame de Stael's "Corinne." I wonder what they talk about at night when we are all asleep. Here is another happy juxtaposition : old Clarendon next to a modern metaphysician whom he would positively loathe. Here is Sadler next to Malthus, and Horsley next to Priestley ; but this sort of thing happens most in the best regulated libraries. It is a charming reflection for controversial writers, that their works will be put together on the same shelves, often between the same covers; and that, in the minds of educated men, the name of one writer will be sure to recall the name of the other. So they go down to posterity as a brotherhood.

Milverton. To complete Ellesmere's theory, we may say that all those injuries to books which we choose to throw upon some wretched worm, are but the wounds from rival books.

Ellesmere. Certainly. But now let us proceed to polish up the weapons of another of these spiteful creatures.

Dunsford. Yes. What is to be our essay to-day, Milverton ?

Milverton. Fiction.

Ellesmere. Now, that is really unfortunate. Fiction is just the subject to be discussed—no, not discussed, talked over—out of doors on a hot day, all of us lying about in easy attitudes on the grass, Dunsford with his gaiters forming a most picturesque and prominent figure. But there is nothing complete in this life.

"Surgit amari aliquid:" and so we must listen to
Fiction in arm-chairs.

FICTION.

The influence of works of fiction is unbounded.
Even the minds of well-informed people are often
more stored with characters from acknowledged fiction
than from history or biography, or the real life around
them. We dispute about these characters as if they
were realities. Their experience is our experience;
we adopt their feelings, and imitate their acts. And
so there comes to be something traditional even in the
management of the passions. Shakespeare's historical
plays were the only history to the Duke of Marlborough. Thousands of Greeks acted under the influence of what Achilles or Ulysses did, in Homer.
The poet sings of the deeds that shall be. He imagines
the past; he forms the future.

Yet how surpassingly interesting is real life when
we get an insight into it. Occasionally a great genius
lifts up the veil of history, and we see men who once
really were alive, who did not always live only in
history; or, amidst the dreary page of battles, levies,
sieges, and the sleep-inducing weavings and unweavings
of political combination, we come, ourselves, across some
spoken or written words of the great actors of the time,
and are then fascinated by the life and reality of these
things. Could you have the life of any man really
portrayed to you, sun-drawn as it were, its hopes, its
fears, its revolutions of opinion in each day, its most
anxious wishes attained, and then, perhaps, crystallising

into its blackest regrets—such a work would go far
to contain all histories, and be the greatest lesson
of love, humility, [and tolerance, that men had ever
read.

Now fiction does attempt something like the above.
In history we are cramped by impertinent facts that
must, however, be set down; by theories that must be
answered; evidence that must be weighed; views that
must be taken. Our facts constantly break off just
where we should wish to examine them most closely.
The writer of fiction follows his characters into the
recesses of their hearts. There are no closed doors for
him. His puppets have no secrets from their master.
He plagues you with no doubts, no half-views, no
criticism. Thus they thought, he tells you; thus they
looked, thus they acted. Then, with every opportunity
for scenic arrangement (for though his characters are
confidential with him, he is only as confidential with
his reader as the interest of the story will allow), it is
not [to be wondered at that the majority of readers
should look upon history as a task, but tales of fiction
as a delight.

The greatest merit of fiction is the one so ably put
forward by Sir James Mackintosh, namely, that it creates
and nourishes sympathy. It extends this sympathy,
too, in directions where, otherwise, we hardly see when
it would have come. But it may be objected that this
sympathy is indiscriminate, and that we are in danger
of mixing up virtue and vice, and blurring both, if we
are led to sympathise with all manner of wrong-doers.
But, in the first place, virtue and vice are so mixed in

real life, that it is well to be somewhat prepared for that fact; and, moreover, the sympathy is not wrongly directed. Who has not felt intense sympathy for Macbeth? Yet could he be alive again, with evil thoughts against "the gracious Duncan," and could he see into all that has been felt for him, would that be an encouragement to murder? The intense pity of wise people for the crimes of others, when rightly represented, is one of the strongest antidotes against crime. We have taken the extreme case of sympathy being directed towards bad men. How often has fiction made us sympathise with obscure suffering and retiring greatness, with the world-despised, and especially with those mixed characters in whom we might otherwise see but one colour—with Shylock and with Hamlet, with Jeanie Deans and with Claverhouse, with Sancho Panza as well as with Don Quixote.

On the other hand, there is a danger of too much converse with fiction leading us into dream-land, or rather into lubber-land. Of course this "too much converse" implies large converse with inferior writers. Such writers are too apt to make life as they would have it for themselves. Sometimes, also, they must make it to suit booksellers' rules. Having such power over their puppets they abuse it. They can kill these puppets, change their natures suddenly, reward or punish them so easily, that it is no wonder they are led to play fantastic tricks with them. Now, if a sedulous reader of the works of such writers should form his notions of real life from them, he would occasionally meet with rude shocks when he encountered the realities of that life.

For my own part, notwithstanding all the charms of life in swiftly-written novels, I prefer real life. It is true that, in the former, everything breaks off round, every little event tends to some great thing, everybody one meets is to exercise some great influence for good or ill upon one's fate. I take it for granted one fancies oneself the hero. Then all one's fancy is paid in ready money, or at least one can draw upon it at the end of the third volume. One leaps to remote wealth and honour by hairbreadth chances; and one's uncle in India always dies opportunely. To be sure the thought occurs, that if this novel life could be turned into real life, one might be the uncle in India and not the hero of the tale. But that is a trifling matter, for at any rate one should carry on with spirit somebody else's story. On the whole, however, as I said before, I prefer real life, where nothing is tied up neatly, but all in odds and ends; where the doctrine of compensation enters largely, where we are often most blamed when we least deserve it, where there is no third volume to make things straight, and where many an Augustus marries many a Belinda, and, instead of being happy ever afterwards, finds that there is a growth of trials and troubles for each successive period of man's life.

In considering the subject of fiction, the responsibility of the writers thereof is a matter worth pointing out. We see clearly enough that historians are to be limited by facts and probabilities; but we are apt to make a large allowance for the fancies of writers of fiction. We must remember, however, that fiction is not falsehood. If a writer puts abstract virtues into book-clothing, and sends them upon stilts into the world, he is a bad writer: if he classifies men, and attributes all virtue to one class and all vice to another, he is a false writer. Then, again, if his ideal is so poor, that he fancies man's welfare to consist in immediate happiness; if he means to paint a great man and paints only a greedy one, he is a mischievous writer : and not the less so, although by lamplight and amongst a juvenile audience, his coarse scene-painting should be thought very grand. He may be true to his own fancy, but he is false to Nature. A writer, of course, cannot get beyond his own ideal : but at least he should see that he works up to it : and if it is a poor one, he had better write histories of the utmost concentration of dulness, than amuse us with unjust and untrue imaginings.

Ellesmere. I am glad you have kept to the obvious things about fiction. It would have been a great nuisance to have had to follow you through intricate theories about what fiction consists in, and what are its limits, and so on. Then we should have got into questions touching the laws of representation generally, and then into art, of which, between ourselves, you know very little.

Dunsford. Talking of representation, what do you

two. who have now seen something of the world, think about representative government ?

Ellesmere. Dunsford plumps down upon us sometimes with awful questions : what do you think of all philosophy ? or what is your opinion of life in general ? Could not you throw in a few small questions of that kind, together with your representative one, and we might try to answer them all at once. Dunsford is only laughing at us, Milverton.

Milverton. No, I know what was in Dunsford's mind when he asked that question. He has had his doubts and misgivings, when he has been reading a six nights' debate (for the people in the country I daresay do read those things), whether representative government is the most complete device the human mind could suggest for getting at wise rulers.

Ellesmere. It is a doubt which has crossed my mind.

Milverton. And mine ; but the doubt, if it has ever been more than mere petulance, has not had much practical weight with me. Look how the business of the world is managed. There are a few people who think out things, and a few who execute. The former are not to be secured by any device. They are gifts. The latter may be well chosen, have often been well chosen, under other forms of government than the representative one. I believe that the favourites of kings have been a superior race of men. Even a fool does not choose a fool for a favourite. He knows better than that : he must have something to lean against. But between the thinkers and the doers (if, indeed, we ought to make such a distinction), *what a number of useful links there are in a representative government* on account of the much larger number of people admitted into some share of government. What general cultivation must come from that, and what security ! Of course, everything has its wrong side ; and from this number of people let in there comes declamation and claptrap and mob-service, which is much the same thing as courtiership was in other times　But then, to make the comparison a fair one, you must take the wrong side of any other form of government that has been devised.

Dunsford. Well, but so much power centring in the lower house of Parliament, and the getting into Parliament being a thing which is not very inviting to the kind of people one would most like to see there, do you not think that the ablest men are kept away?

Milverton. Yes; but if you make your governing body a unit or a ten, or any small number, how is this power, unless it is Argus-eyed, and myriad-minded, and right-minded too, to choose the right men any better than they are found now? The great danger, as it appears to me, of representative government is lest it should slide down from representative government to delegate government. In my opinion, the welfare of England, in great measure, depends upon what takes place at the hustings. If, in the majority of instances, there were abject conduct there, electors and elected would be alike debased ; upright public men could not be expected to arise from such beginnings ; and thoughtful persons would begin to consider whether some other form of government could not forthwith be made out.

Ellesmere. I have a supreme disgust for the man who at the hustings has no opinion beyond or above the clamour round him. How such a fellow would have kissed the ground before a Pompadour, or waited for hours in a Buckingham's antechamber, only to catch the faintest beam of reflected light from royalty.

But I declare we have been just like schoolboys talking about forms of government and so on.

> "For forms of government let fools contest,
>   That which is *worst* administered is best,"—

that is, representative government.

Milverton. I should not like either of you to fancy, from what I have been saying about representative government, that I do not see the dangers and the evils of it. In fact, it is a frequent thought with me of what importance the House of Lords is at present, and of how much greater importance it might be made. If there were Peers for life, and official members of the House of Commons, it would, I think, meet most of your objections, Dunsford.

Dunsford. I suppose I am becoming a little rusty and disposed to grumble, as I grow old; but there is a good deal in modern government which seems to me very rude and absurd. There comes a clamour, partly reasonable; power is deaf to it, overlooks it, says there is no such thing; then great clamour; after a time, power welcomes that, takes it to its arms, says that now it is loud it is very wise, wishes it had always been clamour itself.

Ellesmere. How many acres do you farm, Dunsford? How spiteful you are!

Dunsford. I am not thinking of Corn Laws alone, as you fancy, Master Ellesmere. But to go to other things. I quite agree, Milverton, with what you were saying just now about the business of the world being carried on by few, and the thinking few being in the nature of gifts to the world, not elicited by King or Kaiser.

Milverton. The mill-streams that turn the clappers of the world arise in solitary places.

Ellesmere. Not a bad metaphor, but untrue. Aristotle, Bacon——

Milverton. Well, I believe it would be much wiser to say, that we cannot lay down rules about the highest work; either when it is done, where it will be done, or how it can be made to be done. It is too immaterial for our measurement; for the highest part even of the mere business of the world is in dealing with ideas. It is very amusing to observe the misconceptions of men on these points. They call for what is outward—can understand that, can praise it. Fussiness and the forms of activity in all ages get great praise. Imagine an active, bustling little prætor under Augustus, how he probably pointed out Horace to his sons as a moony kind of man, whose ways were much to be avoided, and told them it was a weakness in Augustus to like such idle men about him instead of men of business.

Ellesmere. Or fancy a bustling Glasgow merchant of

Adam Smith's day watching him. How little would the merchant have dreamt what a number of vessels were to be floated away by the ink in the Professor's inkstand; and what crashing of axes, and clearing of forests in distant lands, the noise of his pen upon the paper portended.

Milverton. It is not only the effect of the still-working man that the busy man cannot anticipate, but neither can he comprehend the present labour. If Horace had told my prætor that

"Abstinuit Venere et vino, sudavit et alsit,"

"What, to write a few lines!" would his prætorship have cried out. "Why, I can live well and enjoy life; and I flatter myself no one in Rome does more business."

Dunsford. All of it only goes to show how little we know of each other, and how tolerant we ought to be of others' efforts.

Milverton. The trials that there must be every day without any incident that even the most minute household chronicler could set down: the labours without show or noise !

Ellesmere. The deep things that there are which, with unthinking people, pass for shallow things, merely because they are clear as well as deep. My fable of the other day, for instance—which instead of producing any moral effect upon you two, only seemed to make you both inclined to giggle.

Milverton. I am so glad you reminded me of that. I, too, fired with a noble emulation, have invented a fable since we last met which I want you to hear. I assure you I did not mean to laugh at yours : it was only that it came rather unexpectedly upon me. You are not exactly the person from whom one should expect fables.

Dunsford. Now for the fable.

Milverton. There was a gathering together of creatures hurtful and terrible to man, to name their king. Blight, mildew, darkness, mighty waves, fierce winds, Will-o'-the-wisps, and shadows of grim objects, told fearfully their doings and preferred their claims, none prevailing. But when evening came on, a thin mist curled up, derisively, amidst the assemblage, and said, "I gather round a man going to his own home over paths made by his daily footsteps ; and he becomes at once helpless and tame as a child. The lights meant to assist him, then betray. You find him wandering, or need the aid of other Terrors to subdue him. I am, alone, confusion to him.". And all the assemblage bowed before the mist, and made it king, and set it on the brow of many a mountain, where, when it is not doing evil, it may be often seen to this day.

Dunsford. Well, I like that fable : only I am not quite clear about the meaning.

Ellesmere. You had no doubt about mine.

Dunsford. Is the mist calumny, Milverton ?

Ellesmere. No, prejudice, I am sure.

Dunsford. Familiarity with the things around us, obscuring knowledge ?

Milverton. I would rather not explain. Each of you make your own fable of it.

Dunsford. Well, if ever I make a fable, it shall be

one of the old-fashioned sort. with animals for the speakers, and a good easy moral.

Ellesmere. Not a thing requiring the notes of seven German metaphysicians. I must go and talk a little to my friends the trees, and see if I can get any explanation from them. It is turning out a beautiful day after all, notwithstanding my praise of its solidity.

CHAPTER VII.

WE met as usual at our old spot on the lawn for our next reading. I forget what took place before reading, except that Ellesmere was very jocose about our reading "Fiction" in-doors, and the following "November Essay," as he called it, "under a jovial sun. and with the power of getting up and walking away from each other to any extent."

ON THE ART OF LIVING WITH OTHERS.

The " Iliad " for war; the " Odyssey " for wandering; but where is the great domestic epic? Yet it is but commonplace to say, that passions may rage round a tea-table, which would not have misbecome men dashing at one another in war-chariots; and evolutions of patience and temper are performed at the fireside, worthy to be compared with the Retreat of the Ten Thousand. Men have worshipped some fantastic being for living alone in a wilderness; but social martyrdoms place no saints upon the calendar.

We may blind ourselves to it if we like, but the

hatreds and disgusts that there are behind friendship, relationship, service, and, indeed, proximity of all kinds, is one of the darkest spots upon earth. The various relations of life, which bring people together, cannot, as we know, be perfectly fulfilled except in a state where there will, perhaps, be no occasion for any of them. It is no harm, however, to endeavour to see whether there are any methods which may make these relations in the least degree more harmonious now.

In the first place, if people are to live happily together, they must not fancy, because they are thrown together now, that all their lives have been exactly similar up to the present time, that they started exactly alike, and that they are to be for the future of the same mind. A thorough conviction of the difference of men is the great thing to be assured of in social knowledge : it is to life what Newton's law is to astronomy. Sometimes men have a knowledge of it with regard to the world in general : they do not expect the outer world to agree with them in all points, but are vexed at not being able to drive their own tastes and opinions into those they live with. Diversities distress them. They will not see that there are many forms of virtue and wisdom. Yet we might as well say, " Why all these stars ; why this difference ; why not all one star ? "

Many of the rules for people living together in peace follow from the above. For instance, not to interfere unreasonably with others, not to ridicule their tastes, not to question and re-question their resolves, not to indulge in perpetual comment on their proceedings, and to delight in their having other pursuits than ours, are all based upon a thorough perception of the simple fact that they are not we.

Another rule for living happily with others is to avoid having stock subjects of disputation. It mostly happens, when people live much together, that they come to have certain set topics, around which, from frequent dispute, there is such a growth of angry words, mortified vanity, and the like, that the original subject of difference becomes a standing subject for quarrel; and there is a tendency in all minor disputes to drift down to it.

Again, if people wish to live well together, they must not hold too much to logic, and suppose that everything is to be settled by sufficient reason. Dr. Johnson saw this clearly with regard to married people, when he said, " Wretched would be the pair above all names of wretchedness, who should be doomed to adjust by reason every morning all the minute detail of a domestic day." But the application should be much more general than he made it. There is no time for such reasonings, and nothing that is worth them. And when we recollect how two lawyers, or two politicians, can go on contending, and that there is no end of one-sided reasoning on any subject, we shall not be sure that such contention is the best mode for arriving at truth. But certainly it is not the way to arrive at good temper.

If you would be loved as a companion, avoid unnecessary criticism upon those with whom you live. The number of people who have taken out judges' patents for themselves is very large in any society. Now it would be hard for a man to live with another who was always criticising his actions, even if it were kindly and just criticism. It would be like living between the glasses of a microscope. But these self-elected judges, like their prototypes, are very apt to have the persons they judge brought before them in the guise of culprits.

One of the most provoking forms of the criticism above alluded to is that which may be called criticism over the shoulder. "Had I been consulted," "Had you listened to me," "But you always will," and such short scraps of sentences may remind many of us of dissertations which we have suffered and inflicted, and of which we cannot call to mind any soothing effect.

Another rule is, not to let familiarity swallow up all courtesy. Many of us have a habit of saying to those with whom we live such things as we say about strangers behind their backs. There is no place, however, where real politeness is of more value than where we mostly think it would be superfluous. You may say more truth, or rather speak out more plainly, to your associates, but not less courteously than you do to strangers.

Again, we must not expect more from the society of our friends and companions than it can give, and especially must not expect contrary things. It is something arrogant to talk of travelling over other minds (mind being, for what we know, infinite); but still we become familiar with the upper views, tastes, and tempers of our associates. And it is hardly in man to estimate justly what is familiar to him. In travelling along at night, as Hazlitt says, we catch a glimpse into cheerful-looking rooms with light blazing in them, and we conclude involuntarily how happy the inmates must be. Yet there is heaven and hell in those rooms—the same heaven and hell that we have known in others.

There are two great classes of promoters of social happiness—cheerful people, and people who have some reticence. The latter are more secure benefits to society even than the former. They are non-conductors of all the heats and animosities around them. To have peace in a house, or a family, or any social circle, the members of it must beware of passing on hasty and uncharitable speeches, which, the whole of the context seldom being told, is often not conveying but creating mischief. They must be very good people to avoid doing this; for let Human Nature say what it will, it likes sometimes to look on at a quarrel, and that not altogether from ill-nature, but from a love of excitement, for the same reason that Charles II. liked to attend the debates in the Lords, because they were " as good as a play."

We come now to the consideration of temper, which might have been expected to be treated first. But to cut off the means and causes of bad temper is, perhaps, of as much importance as any direct dealing with the temper itself. Besides, it is probable that in small social circles there is more suffering from unkindness than ill-temper. Anger is a thing that those who live under us suffer more from than those who live with us. But all the forms of ill-humour and sour-sensitiveness, which especially belong to equal intimacy (though indeed, they are common to all), are best to be met by impassiveness. When two sensitive persons are shut up together, they go on vexing each other with a reproductive irritability.* But sensitive and hard people get on well together. The supply of temper is not altogether out of the usual laws of supply and demand.

Intimate friends and relations should be careful when they go out into the world together, or admit others to their own circle, that they do not make a bad use of the knowledge which they have gained of each other by their intimacy. Nothing is more common than this, and did it not mostly proceed from mere carelessness, it would be superlatively ungenerous. You seldom need wait for the written life of a man to hear about his weaknesses, or what are supposed to be

* Madame Necker de Saussure's maxim about firmness with children has suggested the above. "Ce que plie ne peut servir d'appui, et l'enfant veut être appuyé. Non-seulement il en a besoin, mais il le désire, mais sa tendresse la plus constante n'est qu'à ce prix. Si vous lui faites l'effet d'un autre enfant, si vous partagez ses passions, ses vacillations continuelles, si vous lui rendez tous ses mouvements en les augmentant, soit par la contrariété, soit par un excès de complaisance, il pourra se servir de vous comme d'un jouet, mais non être heureux en votre présence ; il pleurera, se mutinera, et bientôt le souvenir d'un temps de désordre et d'humeur se liera avec votre idée. Vous n'avez pas été le soutien de votre enfant, vous ne l'avez pas préservé de cette fluctuation perpétuelle de la volonté, maladie des êtres faibles et livrés à une imagination vive ; vous n'avez assuré ni sa paix, ni sa sagesse, ni son bonheur. pourquoi vous croirait-il sa mère."—*L'Education Progressive*, vol. i., p. 228.

such, if you know his intimate friends, or meet him in company with them.

Lastly, in conciliating those we live with, it is most surely done, not by consulting their interests, nor by giving way to their opinions, so much as by not offending their tastes. The most refined part of us lies in this region of taste, which is perhaps a result of our whole being rather than a part of our nature, and, at any rate, is the region of our most subtle sympathies and antipathies.

It may be said that if the great principles of Christianity were attended to, all such rules, suggestions, and observations as the above would be needless. True enough! Great principles are at the bottom of all things; but to apply them to daily life, many little rules, precautions, and insights are needed. Such things hold a middle place between real life and principles, as form does between matter and spirit, moulding the one and expressing the other.

Ellesmere. Quite right that last part. Everybody must have known really good people, with all Christian temper, but having so little Christian prudence as to do a great deal of mischief in society.

Dunsford. There is one case, my dear Milverton, which I do not think you have considered: the case where people live unhappily together, not from any bad relations between them, but because they do not agree about the treatment of others. A just person, for instance, who would bear anything for himself or herself, must remonstrate, at the hazard of any disagreement, at injustice to others.

Milverton. Yes. That, however, is a case to be decided upon higher considerations than those I have been treating of. A man must do his duty in the way of preventing injustice, and take what comes of it.

Ellesmere. For people to live happily together, the real secret is that they should not live too much together. Of course, you cannot say that; it would sound harsh, and cut short the essay altogether.

Again, you talk about tastes and "region of subtle sympathies," and all that. I have observed that if people's vanity is pleased, they live well enough together. Offended vanity is the great separator. You hear a man (call him B) saying that he is really not himself before So-and-so; tell him that So-and-so admires him very much and is himself rather abashed before B, and B is straightway comfortable, and they get on harmoniously together, and you hear no more about subtle sympathies or antipathies.

Dunsford. What a low view you do take of things sometimes, Ellesmere!

Milverton. I should not care how low it was, but it is not fair—at least, it does not contain the whole matter. In the very case he has put, there was a subtle embarrassment between B and So-and-so. Well, now, let these people not merely meet occasionally, but be obliged to live together, without any such explanation as Ellesmere has imagined, and they will be very uncomfortable from causes that you cannot impute to vanity. It takes away much of the savour of life to live amongst those with whom one has not anything like one's fair value. It may not be mortified vanity, but unsatisfied sympathy, which causes this discomfort. B thinks that the other does not know him; he feels that he has no place with the other. When there is intense admiration on one side, there is hardly a care in the mind of the admiring one as to what estimation he is held in. But, in ordinary cases, some clearly defined respect and acknowledgment of worth is needed on both sides. See how happy a man is in any office or service who is acknowledged to do something well. How comfortable he is with his superiors! He has his place. It is not exactly a satisfaction of his vanity, but an acknowledgment of his useful existence that contents him. I do not mean to say that there are not innumerable claims for acknowledgment of merit and service made by rampant vanity and egotism, which claims cannot be satisfied, ought not to be satisfied, and which, being unsatisfied, embitter people. But I think your word Vanity will not explain all the feelings we have been talking about.

Ellesmere. Perhaps not.

Dunsford. Certainly not.

Ellesmere. Well, at any rate, you will admit that there is a class of dreadfully humble people who make immense claims at the very time that they are explaining that they have no claims. They say they know they cannot be esteemed; they are well aware that they are not wanted, and so on, all the while making it a sort of grievance and a claim that they are not what they know themselves not to be; whereas, if they did but fall back upon their humility, and keep themselves quiet about their demerits, they would be strong then, and in their place and happy, doing what they could.

Milverton. It must be confessed that these people do make their humility somewhat obnoxious. Yet, after all, you allow that they know their deficiencies, and they only say, " I know I have not much to recommend me, but I wish to be loved, nevertheless."

Ellesmere. Ah, if they only said it a few times ! Besides, there is a little envy mixed up with the humility that I mean.

Dunsford. Travelling is a great trial of people's ability to live together.

Ellesmere. Yes. Lavater says that you do not know a man until you have divided an inheritance with him ; but I think a long journey with him will do.

Milverton. Well, and what is it in travelling that makes people disagree ? Not direct selfishness, but injudicious management; stupid regrets, for instance, at things not being different from what they are, or from what they might have been, if " the other route " had been chosen; fellow-travellers punishing each other with each other's tastes ; getting stock subjects of disputation ; laughing unseasonably at each other's vexations and discomforts ; and endeavouring to settle everything by the force of sufficient reason, instead of by some authorised will, or by tossing up. Thus, in the short time of a journey, almost all modes and causes of human disagreement are brought into action.

D—212

Ellesmere. My favourite one not being the least—over-much of each other's company.

For my part, I think one of the greatest bores of companionship is, not merely that people wish to fit tastes and notions on you just as they might the first pair of ready-made shoes they meet with, a process amusing enough to the bystander, but exquisitely uncomfortable to the person being ready-shod: but that they bore you with never-ending talk about their pursuits, even when they know that you do not work in the same groove with them, and that they cannot hope to make you do so.

Dunsford. Nobody can accuse you of that fault, Ellesmere: I never heard you dilate much upon any-thing that interested you, though I have known you have some pet subject, and to be working at it for months. But this comes of your coldness of nature.

Ellesmere. Well, it might bear a more favourable construction. But to go back to the essay. It only contemplates the fact of people living together as equals, if we may so say; but in general, of course, you must add some other relationship or connection than that of merely being together.

Milverton. I had not overlooked that; but there are certain general rules in the matter that may be applied to nearly all relationship, just as I have taken that one from Johnson, applied by him to married life, about not endeavouring to settle all things by reasoning, and have given it a general application which, I believe, it will bear.

Ellesmere. There is one thing that I should think

must often make women very unreasonable and unpleasant companions. Oh, you may both hold up your hands and eyes, but I am not married, and can say what I please. Of course you put on the proper official look of astonishment; and I will duly report it. But I was going to say that Chivalry, which has doubtless done a great deal of good, has also done a great deal of harm. Women may talk the greatest unreason out of doors, and nobody kindly informs them that it is unreason. They do not talk much before clever men, and when they do, their words are humoured and dandled as children's sayings are. Now, I should fancy —mind, I do not want either of you to say that my fancy is otherwise than quite unreasonable—I should fancy that when women have to hear reason at home it must sound odd to them. The truth is, you know, we cannot pet anything much without doing it mischief. You cannot pet the intellect, any more than the will, without injuring it. Well then, again, if you put people upon a pedestal and do a great deal of worship around them, I cannot think but the will in such cases must become rather corrupted, and that lessons of obedience must fall rather harshly——

Dunsford. Why, you Mahometan, you Turk of a lawyer—would you do away with all the high things of courtesy, tenderness for the weaker, and——

Milverton. No, I see what he means, and there is something in it. Many a woman is brought up in unreason and self-will from these causes that he has given, as many a man from other causes ; but there is one great corrective that he has omitted, and which is, that all forms, fashions, and outward things have a tendency to go down before realities when they come hand to hand together. Knowledge and judgment prevail. Governing is apt to fall to the right person in private as in public affairs.

Ellesmere. Those who give way in public affairs, and let the men who can do a thing do it, are so far wise that they know what is to be done, mostly. But the very things I am arguing against are the unreason and self-will, which being constantly pampered, do not appreciate reason or just sway. Besides, is there not a force in ill-humour and unreason to which you constantly see the wisest bend? You will come round to my opinion some day. I do not want, though, to convince you. It is no business of mine.

Milverton. Well, I may be wrong, but I think, when we come to consider education, I can show you how the dangers you fear may be greatly obviated, without Chivalry being obliged to put on a wig and gown, and be wise.

Dunsford. Meanwhile, let us enjoy the delightful atmosphere of courtesy, unreasonable sometimes, if you like, which saves many people being put down with the best arguments in the most convincing manner, or being weighed, estimated, and given way to, so as not to spoil them.

Ellesmere. Do not tell, either of you, what I have been saying. I shall always be poked up into some garret when I come to see you, if you do.

Dunsford. I thing the most curious thing, as regards people living together, is the intense ignorance they sometimes are in of each other. Many years ago, one or other of you said something of this kind to me, and I have often thought of it since.

Milverton. People fulfil a relation towards each other, and they only know each other in that relation, especially if it is badly managed by the superior one; but any way the relationship involves some ignorance. They perform orbits round each other, each gyrating, too, upon his own axis, and there are parts of the character of each which are never brought into view of the other.

Ellesmere. I should carry this notion of yours, Milverton, farther than you do. There is a peculiar mental relation soon constituted between associates of any kind, which confines and prevents complete knowledge on both sides. Each man, in some measure therefore, knows others only through himself. Tennyson makes Ulysses say,

"I am a part of all that I have seen;"

it might have run,

"I am a part of all that I have heard."

Dunsford. Ellesmere becoming metaphysical and transcendental!

Ellesmere. Well, well, we will leave these heights, and descend in little drops of criticism. There are two or three things you might have pointed out, Milverton. Perhaps you would say that they are included in what you have said, but I think not. You talk of the mischief of much comment on each other amongst those who live together. You might have shown, I think, that in the case of near friends and relations this comment also deepens into interference—at least it partakes of that nature. Friends and relations should, therefore, be especially careful to avoid needless comments on each other. They do just the contrary. That is one of the reasons why they often hate one another so much.

Dunsford. Ellesmere!

Ellesmere. Protest, if you like, my dear Dunsford.

Dissentient,

1. Because I wish it were not so.
2. Because I am sorry that it is.

(Signed) DUNSFORD.

Milverton. "Hate" is too strong a word, Ellesmere; what you say would be true enough, if you would put "are not in sympathy with."

Ellesmere. "Have a quiet distaste for." That is the proper medium. Now, to go to another matter. You have not put the case of over-managing people, who are tremendous to live with.

Milverton. I have spoken about "interfering unreasonably with others."

Ellesmere. That does not quite convey what I mean. It is when the manager and the managee are both of the same mind as to the thing to be done; but the former insists, and instructs, and suggests, and foresees, till the other feels that all free agency for him is gone.

Milverton. It is a sad thing to consider how much of their abilities people turn to tiresomeness. You

see a man who would be very agreeable if he were
not so observant: another who would be charming, if
he were deaf and dumb: a third delightful, if he did
not vex all around him with superfluous criticism.

Ellesmere. A hit at me that last, I suspect. But I
shall go on. You have not, I think, made enough
merit of independence in companionship. If I were to
put into an aphorism what I mean, I should say,
Those who depend wholly on companionship are the
worst companions ; or thus : Those deserve companionship who can do without it. There, Mr. Aphoriser
General, what do you say to that?

Milverton. Very good, but——

Ellesmere. Of course a "but" to other people's
aphorisms, as if every aphorism had not buts innumerable. We critics, you know, cannot abide criticism.
We do all the criticism that is needed ourselves. I
wonder at the presumption sometimes of you wretched
authors. But to proceed. You have not said anything about the mischief of superfluous condolence
amongst people who live together. I flatter myself
that I could condole anybody out of all peace of mind.

Milverton. All depends upon whether condolence
goes with the grain, or against the grain, of vanity. I
know what you mean, however: For instance, it is a
very absurd thing to fret much over other people's
courses, not considering the knowledge and discipline
that there is in any course that a man may take.
And it is still more absurd to be constantly showing
the people fretted over that you are fretting over
them. I think a good deal of what you call superfluous

condolence would come under the head of superfluous criticism.

Ellesmere. Not altogether. In companionship, when an evil happens to one of the circle, the others should simply attempt to share and lighten it, not to expound it, or dilate on it, or make it the least darker. The person afflicted generally apprehends all the blackness sufficiently. Now, unjust abuse by the world is to me like the howling of the wind at night when one is warm within. Bring any draught of it into one's house though, and it is not so pleasant.

Dunsford. Talking of companionship, do not you think there is often a peculiar feeling of home where age or infirmity is? The arm-chair of the sick or the old is the centre of the house. They think, perhaps, that they are unimportant; but all the household hopes and cares flow to them and from them.

Milverton. I quite agree with you. What you have just depicted is a beautiful sight, especially when, as you often see, the age or infirmity is not in the least selfish or exacting.

Ellesmere. We have said a great deal about the companionship of human beings; but, upon my word, we ought to have kept a few words for our dog friends. Rollo has been lolling out his great tongue, and looking wistfully from face to face, as we each began our talk. A few minutes ago he was quite concerned, thinking I was angry with you, when I would not let you " but " my aphorism. I am not sure which of the three I should rather go out walking with now: Dunsford, Rollo, Milverton. The middle one is the safest companion. I am sure not to get out of humour with him. But I have no objection to try the whole three : only I vote for much continuity of silence, as we have had floods of discussion to-day.

Dunsford. Agreed!

Ellesmere. Come, Rollo, you may bark now, as you have been silent, like a wise dog, all the morning.

CHAPTER VIII.

IT was arranged, during our walk, that Ellesmere should come and stay a day or two with me, and see the neighbouring cathedral, which is nearer my house than Milverton's. The visit over, I brought him back to Worth-Ashton. Milverton saw us coming, walked down the hill to meet us, and after the usual greetings, began to talk to Ellesmere.

Milverton. So you have been to see our cathedral. I say " our," for when a cathedral is within ten miles of us, we feel a property in it, and are ready to battle for its architectural merits.

Ellesmere. You know I am not a man to rave about cathedrals.

Milverton. I certainly do not expect you to do so. To me a cathedral is mostly somewhat of a sad sight. You have Grecian monuments, if anything so misplaced can be called Grecian, imbedded against and cutting into Gothic pillars ; the doors shut for the greater part of the day ; only a little bit of the building used ; beadledom predominant ; the clink of money here and there ; white-wash in vigour ; the singing indifferent ; the sermons not indifferent but bad ; and some visitors from London forming, perhaps, the most important part of the audience ; in fact, the thing having become a show. We look about, thinking when piety filled every corner, and feel that the cathedral is too big for the Religion which is a dried-up thing that rattles in this empty space.

Ellesmere. This is the boldest simile I have heard for a long time. My theory about cathedrals is very different, I must confess.

Dunsford. Theory !

Ellesmere. Well, "theory" is not the word I ought to have used—feeling then. My feeling is, how strong this creature was, this worship, how beautiful, how alluring, how complete ; but there was something stronger—truth.

Milverton. And more beautiful ?

Ellesmere. Yes, and far more beautiful.

Milverton. Doubtless, to the free spirits who brought truth forward.

Ellesmere. You are only saying this, Milverton, to try what I will say ; but, despite of all sentimentalities, you sympathise with any emancipation of the human mind, as I do, however much the meagreness of Pro-testantism may be at times distasteful to you.

Milverton. I did not say I was anxious to go back. Certainly not. But what says Dunsford ? Let us sit down on this stile and hear what he has to say.

Dunsford. I cannot talk to you about this subject. If I tell you of all the merits (as they seem to me) of the Church of England, you will both pick what I say to pieces, whereas if I leave you to fight on, one or the other will avail himself of those arguments on which our Church is based.

Milverton. Well, Dunsford, you are very candid, and would make a complete diplomatist: truth-telling being now pronounced (rather late in the day) the very acme of diplomacy. But do you not own that our cathedrals are sadly misused?

Dunsford. Now, very likely, if more were made of them, you, and men who think like you, would begin to cry out "superstition"; and would instantly turn round and inveigh against the uses which you now, perhaps, imagine for cathedrals.

Milverton. Well, one never can answer for oneself; but at any rate, I do not see what is the meaning of building new churches in neighbourhoods where there are already the noblest buildings suitable for the same purposes. Is there a church religion, and is there a cathedral religion?

Ellesmere. You cannot make the present fill the garb of the past, Milverton, any more than you could make the past fill that of the present. Now, as regards the very thing you are about to discuss to-day, if it be the same you told us in our last walk—Education: if you are only going to give us some institution for it, I daresay it may be very good for to-day, or for this generation, but it will have its sere and yellow leaf, and there will be a time when future Milvertons, in sentimental mood, will moan over it, and wish they had it and all that has grown up to take its place at the same time. But all this is what I have often heard you say yourself in other words.

Dunsford. This is very hard doctrine, and not quite sound, I think. In getting the new gain, we always sacrifice something, and we should look with some pious regard to what was good in the things which are past. That good is generally one which, though it may not be equal to the present, would make a most valuable supplement to it.

Milverton. I would try and work in the old good thing with the new, not as patchwork though, but making the new thing grow out in such a way as to embrace the old advantage.

Ellesmere. Well, we must have the essay before we branch out into our philosophy. Pleasure afterwards —I will not say what comes first.

EDUCATION.

The word education is so large, that one may almost as well put "world," or "the end and object of being," at the head of an essay. It should, therefore, soon be declared what such a heading does mean. The word education suggests chiefly to some minds what the State can do for those whom they consider its young people—the children of the poorer classes : to others it presents the idea of all the training that can be got for money at schools and colleges, and which can be fairly accomplished and shut in at the age of one-and-twenty. This essay, however, will not be a treatise on government education, or other school and college education, but will only contain a few points in reference to the general subject, which may escape more methodical and enlarged discussions.

In the first place, as regards government education, it must be kept in mind that there is a danger of its being too interfering and formal, of its overlying private enterprise, insisting upon too much uniformity, and injuring local connections and regards. Education, even in the poorest acceptance of the word, is a great thing : but the harmonious intercourse of different ranks, if not a greater, is a more difficult one ; and we must not gain the former at any considerable sacrifice of the latter.

There is another point connected with this branch of the subject which requires, perhaps, to be noted. If government provision is made in any case, might it not be combined with private payment in other cases, or enter in the way of rewards, so as to do good throughout each step of the social ladder? The lowest kind of school education is a power, and it is desirable that the gradations of this power should correspond to other influences which we know to be good. For instance, a hard-working man saves something to educate his children; if he can get a little better education for them than other parents of his own rank for theirs, it is an incentive and a reward to him, and the child's bringing up at home is a thing which will correspond to this better education at school. In this there are the elements at once of stability and progress.

These views may possibly seem too refined, but at any rate they require consideration.

The next branch of the subject is the ordinary education of young persons not of the poorest classes, with which the State has hitherto had little or nothing to do. This may be considered under four heads: religious, moral, intellectual, and physical education. With regard to the first, there is not much that can be put into rules about it. Parents and tutors will naturally be anxious to impress those under their charge with the religious opinions which they themselves hold. In doing this, however, they should not omit to lay a foundation for charity towards people of other religious opinions. For this purpose, it may be requisite to give a child a notion that there are other creeds besides that in which it is brought up itself. And especially, let it not suppose that all good and wise people are of its church or chapel. However desirable it may appear to the person teaching that there should be such a thing as unity of religion, yet as the facts of the world are against his wishes, and as this is the world which the child is to enter, it is well that the child should in reasonable time be informed of these facts. It may be said in reply that history sufficiently informs children on these points. But the world of the young is the domestic circle; all beyond is fabulous, unless brought home to them by comment. The fact, therefore, of different opinions in religious matters being held by good people should sometimes be dwelt upon, instead of being shunned, if we would secure a ground-work of tolerance in a child's mind.

INTELLECTUAL EDUCATION.

In the intellectual part of education there is the absolute knowledge to be acquired, and the ways of acquiring knowledge to be gained. The latter of course form the most important branch. They can, in some measure, be taught. Give children little to do, make much of its being accurately done. This will give accuracy. Insist upon speed in learning, with careful reference to the original powers of the pupil. This speed gives the habit of concentrating attention, one of the most valuable of mental habits. Then cultivate logic. Logic is not the hard matter that is fancied. A young person, especially after a little geometrical training, may soon be taught to perceive where a fallacy exists, and whether an argument is well sustained. It is not, however, sufficient for him to be able to examine sharply and to pull to pieces. He must learn how to build. This is done by method. The higher branches of method cannot be taught at first. But you may begin by teaching orderliness of mind. Collecting, classifying, contrasting and weighing facts, are some of the processes by which method is taught. When these four things, accuracy, attention, logic, and method are attained, the intellect is fairly furnished with its instruments.

As regards the things to be taught, they will vary to some extent in each age. The general course of education pursued at any particular time may not be the wisest by any means, and greatness will overleap it and neglect it, but the mass of men may go more safely and comfortably, if not with the stream, at least by the side of it.

In the choice of studies too much deference should not be paid to the bent of a young person's mind. Excellence in one or two things which may have taken the fancy of a youth (or which really may suit his genius) will ill compensate for a complete ignorance of those branches of study which are very repugnant to him; and which are, therefore, not likely to be learnt when he has freedom in the choice of his studies.

Amongst the first things to be aimed at in the intellectual part of education is variety of pursuit. A human being, like a tree, if it is to attain to perfect symmetry, must have light and air given to it from all quarters. This may be done without making men superficial. Scientific method may be acquired without many sciences being learnt. But one or two great branches of science must be accurately known. So, too, the choice works of antiquity may be thoroughly appreciated without extensive reading. And passing on from mere learning of any kind, a variety of pursuits, even in what may be called accomplishments, is eminently serviceable. Much may be said of the advantage of keeping a man to a few pursuits, and of the great things done thereby in the making of pins and needles. But in this matter we are not thinking of the things that are to be done, but of the persons who are to do them. Not wealth but men. A number of one-sided men may make a great nation, though I much incline to doubt that; but such a nation will not contain a number of great men.

The very advantage that flows from division of labour, and the probable consequences that men's future bread-getting pursuits will be more and more sub-divided, and therefore limited, make it the more necessary that a man should begin life with a broad basis of interest in many things which may cultivate his faculties and develop his nature. This multifarious-ness of pursuit is needed also in the education of the poor. Civilisation has made it easy for a man to brutalise himself: how is this to be counteracted but by endowing him with many pursuits which may distract him from vice? It is not that kind of educa-tion which leads to no employment in after-life that will do battle with vice. But when education enlarges the field of life-long good pursuits, it becomes formid-able to the soul's worst enemies.

MORAL EDUCATION.

In considering moral education we must recollect that there are three agents in this matter—the child himself, the influence of his grown-up friends, and that of his contemporaries. All that his grown-up friends tell him in the way of experience goes for very little, except in palpable matters. They talk of ab-stractions which he cannot comprehend: and the "Arabian Nights" is a truer world to him than that they talk of. Still, though they cannot furnish ex-perience, they can give motives. Indeed, in their daily intercourse with the child, they are always doing so. For instance, truth, courage, and kindness are the great moral qualities to be instilled. Take courage, in its highest form—moral courage.   If a child perpetually hears such phrases (and especially if they are applied to his own conduct), as, " What people will say," " How they will look at you," " What they will think," and the like, it tends to destroy all just self-reliance in that child's mind, and to set up instead an exaggerated notion of public opinion, the greatest tyrant of these times.   People can see this in such an obvious thing as animal courage.   They will avoid over-cautioning children against physical dangers, knowing that the danger they talk much about will become a bug-bear to the child which it may never get rid of.   But a similar peril lurks in the application of moral motives.   Truth, courage, and kindness are likely to be learnt, or not, by children, according as they hear and receive encouragement in the direction of these pre-eminent qualities. When attempt is made to frighten a child with these worldly maxims, " What will be said of you ? " " Are you like such a one ? " and such things, it is meant to draw him under the rule of grown-up respectability. The last thing thought of by the parent or teacher is, that such maxims will bring the child under the especial guidance of the most unscrupulous of his contemporaries.   They will use ridicule and appeal to their little world, which will be his world, and ask, " What will be said " of him.   There should be some stuff in him of his own to meet these awful generalities.

PHYSICAL EDUCATION.

The physical education of children is a very simple matter, too simple to be much attended to without great perseverance and resolution on the part of those who care for the children. It consists, as we all know, in good air, simple diet, sufficient exercise, and judicious clothing. The first requisite is the most important, and by far the most frequently neglected. This neglect is not so unreasonable as it seems. It arises from pure ignorance. If the mass of mankind knew what scientific men know about the functions of the air, they would be as careful in getting a good supply of it as of their other food. All the people that ever were supposed to die of poison in the middle ages, and that means nearly everybody whose death was worth speculating about, are not so many as those who die poisoned by bad air in the course of any given year. Even a slightly noxious thing, which is constant, affecting us every moment of the day, must have considerable influence; but the air we breathe is not a thing that slightly affects us, but one of the most important elements of life. Moreover, children are the most affected by impurity of air. We need not weary ourselves with much statistics to ascertain this. One or two broad facts will assure us of it. In Nottingham there is a district called Byron Ward, " the densest and worst-conditioned quarter of the town." A table has been made by Mr. William Hawksley of the mortality of equal populations in different parts of the town :

" On comparing the diagram No. 1, relating to Park Ward, with the diagram No. 7, relating to Byron Ward, it will be seen that the heavier pressure of the causes of mortality occasions in the latter district such an undue destruction of early life, that towards 100 deaths, however occurring, Byron Ward contributes fifty per cent. more of children under five years of age than the Park Ward, for the former sends sixty children to an early grave, while the latter sends only forty." *

Mr. Hawksley, the former witness alluded to, goes on to say—

" It has been long known that, with increase of years, up to that period of life which has been denominated the second childhood, the human constitution becomes gradually more resistful, and as it were slowly hardened against the repeated attacks of those more acute disorders, incident to an inferior degree of sanitary civilisation, by which large portions of an infant population are continually overcome and rapidly swept away. From the operation of these and more extraneous influences of a disturbing character, an infant population is almost entirely exempted ; and on this account it is considered that an infant population constitutes, as it were, a delicate barometer, from which we may derive more early and more certain indications of the presence and comparative force of *local* causes of mortality and disease than can be obtained from the more general methods of investigation usually pursued."

The above evidence is confirmed by Mr. Toynbee :—

" The disease of hydrocephalus, of water in the brain, so fatal to children, I find associated with symptoms of scrofula, and arising in abundance in these close rooms. I believe water in the brain, in the class of patients whom I visit, to be almost wholly a scrofulous affection."†

* See *Health of Towns Report*, vol. i., p. 336. A similar result may be deduced from a similar table made by the Rev. J. Clay, of Preston. See the same Report and vol., p. 175.

† See *Health of Towns Report*, vol. i., p. 75.

But supposing people aware of the necessity for good air, and therefore for ventilation, what is to be done ? In houses in great towns certainly, and I should say in all houses, some of the care and expense that are devoted to ornamental work, which when done is often a care, a trouble, an eyesore, and a mischief, should be given to modes of ventilation,* sound building, abundant access of light, largeness of sleeping-rooms, and such useful things. Less ormolu and tinsel of all kinds in the drawing-rooms, and sweeter air in the regions above. Similar things may be done for and by the poor.† And it need hardly be said that those people who care for their children, if of any enlightenment at all, will care greatly for the sanitary condition of their neighbourhood generally. At present you will find at many a rich man's door‡ a nuisance which is poisoning the atmosphere that his children are to breathe, but which he could entirely cure for less than one day's ordinary expenses.

I am afraid that ventilation is very little attended to in school-rooms, either for rich or poor. Now it may be deliberately said that there is very little learned in

* See Dr. Arnott's letter, *Claims of Labour*, p. 232.

† By zinc ventilators, for instance, in the windows and openings into the flues at the top of the rooms. See *Health of Towns Report*, 1844, vol. i., pp. 76, 77. Mr. Coulhart's evidence. —*Ibid.*, pp. 307, 308.

‡ There are several thousand gratings to sewers and drains which are utterly useless on account of their position, and positively injurious from their emanations.—Mr. Guthrie's evidence. —*Ibid.*, vol. ii., p. 255.

any school-room that can compensate for the mischief of its being learned in the midst of impure air. This is a thing which parents must look to, for the grown-up people in the school-rooms, though suffering grievously themselves from insufficient ventilation, will be unobservant of it.* In every system of government inspection, ventilation must occupy a prominent part.

The advantage of simple food for children is a thing that people have found out. And as regards exercise, children happily make great efforts to provide a sufficiency of this for themselves. In clothing, the folly and conformity of grown-up people enter again. Loving mothers, in various parts of the world, carry about at present, I believe, and certainly in times past, carried their little children strapped to a board, with nearly as little power of motion as the board itself. Could we get the returns of stunted miserable beings, or of deaths, from this cause, they would be something portentous. Less in degree, but not less fatally absurd in principle, are many of the strappings, bandages, and incipient stays for children amongst us. They are all mischievous. Allow children, at any rate, some freedom of limbs, some opportunity of being graceful and healthy. Give Nature—dear motherly, much-abused Nature—some chance of forming these little ones according to the

---

* Mr. Wood states that the masters and mistresses were generally ignorant of the depressing and unhealthy effects of the atmosphere which surrounded them, and he mentions the case of the mistress of a dame-school who replied, when he pointed out this to her, "that the children thrived best in dirt!"—*Health of Towns Report,* vol. i., pp. 146, 147.

beneficent intentions of Providence, and not according to the angular designs of ill-educated men and women.

I do not say that attention to the above matters of good air, judicious clothing, and freedom from bandages, will absolutely secure health, because these very things may have been so ill attended to in the parents or in the parental stock as to have introduced special maladies; but at least they are the most important objects to be minded now; and, perhaps, the more to be minded in the children of those who have suffered most from neglect in these particulars.

When we are considering the health of children, it is imperative not to omit the importance of keeping their brains fallow, as it were, for several of the first years of their existence. The mischief perpetrated by a contrary course in the shape of bad health, peevish temper, and developed vanity, is incalculable. It would not be just to attribute this altogether to the vanity of parents; they are influenced by a natural fear lest their children should not have all the advantages of other children. Some infant prodigy which is a standard of mischief throughout its neighbourhood misleads them. But parents may be assured that this early work is not by any means all gain, even in the way of work. I suspect it is a loss; and that children who begin their education late, as it would be called, will rapidly overtake those who have been in harness long before them. And what advantage can it be that the child knows more at six years old than its compeers, especially if this is to be gained by a sacrifice of health which may never be regained? There may be some excuse for this early book-work in the case of those children who are to live by manual labour. It is worth while, perhaps, to run the risk of some physical injury to them, having only their early years in which we can teach them book-knowledge. The chance of mischief, too, will be less, being more likely to be counteracted by their after-life. But for a child who has to be at book-work for the first twenty-one years of its life, what folly it is to exhaust in the least the mental energy, which, after all, is its surest implement.

A similar course of argument applies to taking children early to church, and to over-developing their minds in any way. There is no knowing, moreover, the disgust and weariness that may grow up in the minds of young persons from their attention being prematurely claimed. We are now, however, looking at early study as a matter of health; and we may certainly put it down in the same class with impure air, stimulating diet, unnecessary bandages, and other manifest physical disadvantages. Civilised life, as it advances, does not seem to have so much repose in it, that we need begin early in exciting the mind, for fear of the man being too lethargical hereafter.

EDUCATION OF WOMEN.

It seems needful that something should be said specially about the education of women. As regards their intellects they have been unkindly treated—too much flattered, too little respected. They are shut up in a world of conventionalities, and naturally believe that to be the only world. The theory of their education

seems to be, that they should not be made companions
to men, and some would say, they certainly are not.
These critics, however, in the high imaginations they
justly form of what women's society might be to men,
forget, perhaps, how excellent a thing it is already.
Still the criticism is not by any means wholly unjust.
It appears rather as if there had been a falling off since
the olden times in the education of women. A writer
of modern days, arguing on the other side, has said, that
though we may talk of the Latin and Greek of Lady
Jane Grey and Queen Elizabeth, yet we are to consider
that that was the only learning of the time, and that
many a modern lady may be far better instructed,
although she knew nothing of Latin and Greek.
Certain it is, she may know more facts, have read more
books : but this does not assure us that she may not be
less conversable, less companionable. Wherein does
the cultivated and thoughtful man differ from the
common man ? In the method of his discourse. His
questions upon a subject in which he is ignorant are
full of interest. His talk has a groundwork of reason.
This rationality must not be supposed to be dulness.
Folly is dull. Now, would women be less charming if
they had more power, or at least more appreciation, of
reasoning ? Their flatterers tell them that their
intuition is such that they need not man's slow processes
of thought. One would be very sorry to have a grave
question of law that concerned oneself decided upon
by intuitive judges, or a question of fact by intuitive
jurymen. And so of all human things that have to be
canvassed, it is better, and more amusing too, that

they should be discussed according to reason.   Moreover, the exercise of the reasoning faculties gives much
of the pleasure which there is in solid acquirements;
so that the obvious facts in life and history will hardly
be acquired by those who are not in the habit of reasoning upon them.   Hence it comes, that women have less
interest in great topics, and less knowledge of them,
than they might have.

Again, if either sex requires logical education, it is
theirs.   The sharp practice of the world drives some
logic into the most vague of men; women are not so
schooled.

But, supposing the deficiency we have been considering to be admitted, how is it to be remedied?
Women's education must be made such as to ensure
some accuracy and reasoning.   This may be done with
any subject of education, and is done with men, whatever they learn, because they are expected to produce
and use their requirements.   But the greatest object of
intellectual education, the improvement of the mental
powers, is as needful for one sex as the other, and
requires the same means in both sexes.   The same
accuracy, attention, logic, and method that are attempted
in the education of men should be aimed at in that of
women.   This will never be sufficiently attended to, as
there are no immediate and obvious fruits from it.
And, therefore, as it is probable, from the different
career of women to that of men, that whatever women
study will not be studied with the same method and
earnestness as it would be by men, what a peculiar
advantage there is in any study for them, in which no

proficiency whatever can be made without some use of most of the qualities we desire for them. Geometry, for instance, is such a study. It may appear pedantic, but I must confess that Euclid seems to me a book for the young of both sexes. The severe rules upon which the acquisition of the dead languages is built would of course be a great means for attaining the logical habits in question. But Latin and Greek is a deeper pedantry for women than geometry, and much less desirable on many accounts: and geometry would, perhaps, suffice to teach them what reasoning is. I daresay, too, there are accomplishments which might be taught scientifically; and so even the prejudice against the manifest study of science by women be conciliated. But the appreciation of reasoning must be got somehow.

It is a narrow view of things to suppose that a just cultivation of women's mental powers will take them out of their sphere: it will only enlarge that sphere. The most cultivated women perform their common duties best. They see more in those duties. They can do more. Lady Jane Grey would, I daresay, have bound up a wound, or managed a household, with any unlearned woman of her day. Queen Elizabeth did manage a kingdom: and we find no pedantry in her way of doing it.

People who advocate a better training for women must not, necessarily, be supposed to imagine that men and women are by education to be made alike, and are intended to fulfil most of the same offices. There seems reason for thinking that a boundary line exists between the intellects of men and women which, perhaps, cannot be passed over from either side. But, at any rate, taking the whole nature of both sexes, and the inevitable circumstances which cause them to differ, there must be such a difference between men and women that the same intellectual training applied to both would produce most dissimilar results. It has not, however, been proposed in these pages to adopt the same training : and would have been still less likely to be proposed if it could be shown that such training would tend to make men and women unpleasantly similar to each other. The utmost that has been thought of here is to make more of women's faculties, not by any means to translate them into men's—if such a thing were possible, which, we may venture to say, is not. There are some things that are good for all trees—light, air, room—but no one expects by affording some similar advantages of this kind to an oak and a beech, to find them assimilate, though by such means the best of each may be produced.

Moreover, it should be recollected that the purpose of education is not always to foster natural gifts, but sometimes to bring out faculties that might otherwise remain dormant ; and especially so far as to make the persons educated cognisant of excellence in those faculties in others. A certain tact and refinement belong to women, in which they have little to learn from the first : men, too, who attain some portion of these qualities, are greatly the better for them, and I should imagine not less acceptable on that account to women. So, on the other side, there may be an intellectual cultivation for women which may seem a little against the grain, which would not, however, injure any of their peculiar gifts—would, in fact, carry those gifts to the highest, and would increase withal, both to men and women, the pleasure of each other's society.

There is a branch of general education which is not thought at all necessary for women; as regards which, indeed, it is well if they are not brought up to cultivate the opposite. Women are not taught to be courageous. Indeed, to some persons courage may seem as unnecessary for women as Latin and Greek. Yet there are few things that would tend to make women happier in themselves, and more acceptable to those with whom they live, than courage. There are many women of the present day, sensible women in other things, whose panic-terrors are a frequent source of discomfort to themselves and those around them. Now, it is a great mistake to imagine that harshness must go with courage; and that the bloom of gentleness and sympathy must all be rubbed off by that vigour of mind which gives presence of mind, enables a person to be useful in peril, and makes the desire to assist overcome that sickliness of sensibility which can only contemplate distress and difficulty. So far from courage being unfeminine, there is a peculiar grace and dignity in those beings who have little active power of attack or defence, passing through danger with a moral courage which is equal to that of the strongest. We see this in great things. We perfectly appreciate the sweet and noble dignity of an Anne Bullen, a Mary Queen of Scots, or a Marie Antoinette. We see that it is grand for these delicately-bred, high-nurtured, helpless personages to meet Death with a silence and a confidence like his own. But there would be a similar dignity in women's bearing small terrors with fortitude. There is no beauty in fear. It is a mean, ugly, dishevelled creature. No statue can be made of it that a woman would like to see herself like.

Women are pre-eminent in steady endurance of tiresome suffering: they need not be far behind men in a becoming courage to meet that which is sudden and sharp. The dangers and the troubles, too, which we may venture to say they now start at unreasonably, are many of them mere creatures of the imagination—such as, in their way, disturb high-mettled animals brought up to see too little, and therefore frightened at any leaf blown across the road.

We may be quite sure that, without losing any of the most delicate and refined of feminine graces, women may be taught not to give way to unreasonable fears, which should belong no more to the fragile than to the robust.

There is no doubt that courage may in some measure be taught. We agree that the lower kinds of courage are matter of habit, therefore of teaching: and the same thing holds good to some extent of all courage. Courage is as contagious as fear. The saying is, that the brave are the sons and daughters of the brave; but we might as truly say that they must be brought up by the brave. The great novelist, when he wants a coward descended from a valorous race, does well to take him from his clan and bring him up in an unwarlike home.* Indeed, the heroic example of other days

* See "The Fair Maid of Perth."

is in great part the source of courage of each generation ; and men walk up composedly to the most perilous
enterprises, beckoned onwards by the shades of the
brave that were. In civil courage, moral courage, or
courage shown in the minute circumstances of every-
day life, the same law is true. Courage may be
taught by precept, enforced by example, and is good to
be taught to men, women, and children.

EDUCATION TO HAPPINESS.

It is a curious phenomenon in human affairs, that
some of those matters in which education is most
potent should have been amongst the least thought of
as branches of it. What you teach a boy of Latin and
Greek may be good ; but these things are with him but
a little time of each day in his after-life. What you
teach him of direct moral precepts may be very good
seed : it may grow up, especially if it have sufficient
moisture from experience ; but then, again, a man is,
happily, not doing obvious right or wrong all day long.
What you teach him of any bread-getting art may be
of some import to him, as to the quantity and quality
of bread he will get ; but he is not always with his art.
With himself he is always. How important, then, it
is, whether you have given him a happy or a morbid
turn of mind ; whether the current of his life is a clear
wholesome stream, or bitter as Marah. The education
to happiness is a possible thing--not to a happiness
supposed to rest upon enjoyments of any kind, but to
one built upon content and resignation. This is the
best part of philosophy. This enters into the

" wisdom " spoken of in the Scriptures. Now it can be taught. The converse is taught every day and all day long.

To take an example. A sensitive disposition may descend to a child; but it is also very commonly increased, and often created. Captiousness, sensitiveness, and a Martha-like care for the things of this world, are often the direct fruits of education. All these faults of the character, and they are amongst the greatest, may be summed up in a disproportionate care for little things. This is rather a growing evil. The painful neatness and exactness of modern life foster it. Long peace favours it. Trifles become more important, great evils being kept away. And so, the tide of small wishes and requirements gains upon us fully as fast as we can get out of its way by our improved means of satisfying them. Now the unwholesome concern that many parents and governors manifest as to small things must have a great influence on the governed. You hear a child reprimanded about a point of dress, or some trivial thing, as if it had committed a treachery. The criticisms, too, which it hears upon others are often of the same kind. Small omissions, small commissions, false shame, little stumbling-blocks of offence, trifling grievances of the kind that Dr. Johnson, who had known hunger, stormed at Mrs. Thrale for talking about, are made much of; general dissatisfaction is expressed that things are not complete, and that everything in life is not turned out as neat as a Long-Acre carriage; commands are expected to be fulfilled by agents, upon very rapid and incomplete orders, exactly to the mind of the person ordering;—these ways, to which children are very attentive, teach them in their turn to be querulous, sensitive, and full of small cares and wishes. And when you have made a child like this, can you make a world for him that will satisfy him? Tax your civilisation to the uttermost: a punctilious, tiresome disposition expects more. Indeed, Nature, with her vague and flowing ways, cannot at all fit in with a right-angled person. Besides, there are other precise, angular creatures, and these sharp-edged persons wound each other terribly. Of all the things which you can teach people, after teaching them to trust in God, the most important is, to put out of their hearts any expectation of perfection, according to their notions, in this world. This expectation is at the bottom of a great deal of the worldliness we hear so much reprehended, and necessarily gives to little things a most irrational importance.

Observe the effect of this disproportionate care for little things in the disputes of men. A man who does so care, has a garment embroidered with hooks which catch at everything that passes by. He finds many more causes of offence than other men; and each offence is a more bitter thing to him than to others. He does not expect to be offended. Poor man! He goes through life wondering that he is the subject of general attack, and that the world is so quarrelsome.

The result of a bad education in developing undue care for trifles may be seen in its effect on domestic government and government in general. If those in power have this fault, they will make the persons under them miserable by petty, constant blame; or they will make them indifferent to all blame. If this fault is in the governed, they will captiously object to all the ways and plans of their superiors, not knowing the difficulty of doing anything; they will expect miracles of attention, justice, and temper, which the rough-hewed ways of men do not admit of; and they will repine and tease the life out of those in authority. Sometimes both superiors and inferiors, governors and governed, have this fault. This must often happen in a family, and is a fearful punishment to the elders of it. Scarcely any goodness of disposition, and what are called great qualities, can make such difficult materials work well together.

But I end with somewhat of the same argument as I began with, namely, that as a man lives more with himself than with art, science, or even with his fellows, a wise teacher, having before him the intent to make a happy-minded man of his pupil, will try to lay a groundwork of divine contentment in him. If he cannot make him easily pleased, he will at least try and prevent him from being easily disconcerted. Why, even the self-conceit that makes people indifferent to small things, wrapping them in an atmosphere of self-satisfaction, is welcome in a man compared to that querulousness which makes him an enemy to all around. But most commendable is that easiness of mind which is easy because it is tolerant, because it does not look to have everything its own way, because it expects anything but smooth usage in its course here, because it has resolved to manufacture as few miseries out of small evils as can be.

Most of us know what it is to vex our minds because we cannot recall some name or trivial thing which has escaped our memory for the moment. But then we think how foolish this is, what little concern it is to us. We are right in that; yet any defect of memory is a great concern compared to many of the trifling niceties, comforts, offences, and rectangularities which, perhaps, we do not think it an ignoble use of heart and time to waste ourselves upon. It would be well enough to entertain the rabble of small troubles and offences, if we could lay them aside with the delightful facility of children, who, after an agony of tears, are soon found laughing or asleep. But the chagrin and vexation of grown-up people are grown-up too; and, however childish in their origin, are not to be laughed or danced or slept away in childlike simple-heartedness.

We must not imagine that too much stress can well be laid upon the importance of an education to contentment, for it comes under the head of those things which are not adjuncts or acquisitions for a man, but which form the texture of his being. What a man has learnt is of importance; but what he is, what he can do, what he will become, are more significant things. Finally, it may be remarked, that, to make education a great work, we must have the educators great; that book-learning is mainly good as it gives us a chance of coming into the company of greater and better minds than the average of men around us; and that individual greatness and goodness are the things to be aimed at rather than the successful cultivation of those talents which go to form some eminent membership of society. Each man is a drama in himself—has to play all the parts in it; is to be king and rebel, successful and vanquished, free and slave; and needs a bringing-up fit for the universal creature that he is.

Ellesmere. You have been unexpectedly merciful to us. The moment I heard the head of the essay given out, there flitted before my frightened mind volumes of reports, Battersea schools, Bell, Wilderspin, normal farms, National Society, British Schools, interminable questions about how religion might be separated altogether from secular education, or so much religion taught as all religious sects could agree in. These are all very good things and people to discuss, I daresay; but, to tell the truth, the whole subject sits heavy on my soul. I meet a man of inexhaustible dulness, and he talks to me for three hours about some great subject—this very one of education, for instance—till I sit entranced by stupidity, thinking the while, "And this is what we are to become by education—to be like you." Then I see a man like D——, a judicious, reasonable, conversable being, knowing how to be silent too—a man to go through a campaign with—and I find he cannot read or write.

Milverton. This sort of contrast is just the thing to strike you, Ellesmere: and yet you know as well as any of us that to bring forward such contrasts by way of depreciating education would be most unreasonable. There are three things that go to make a man—the education that most people mean by education; then the education that goes deeper, the education of the soul; and, thirdly, a man's gifts of Nature. I agree with all you say about D——; he never says a foolish thing, and does a great many judicious ones. But look what a clever face he has. There are gifts of Nature for you. Then, again, although he cannot read or write, he may have been most judiciously brought up in other respects. He may have had two, therefore, out of the three elements of education. What such instances would show, I believe, if narrowly looked into, is the immense importance of the education of heart and temper.

I feel with you in some measure about the dulness of the subject of education. But then it extends to all things of the institution kind. Men must have a great deal of pedantry, routine, and folly of all sorts, in any large matter they undertake. I had had this feeling for a long time (you know the way in which you have a thing in your mind, although you have never said it out exactly even to yourself)—well, I came upon a passage of Emerson's which I will try to quote, and then I knew what it was that I had felt.

"We are full of mechanical actions. We must needs intermeddle, and have things in our own way, until the sacrifices and virtues of society are odious. Love should make joy; but our benevolence is unhappy. Our Sunday-schools, and churches, and pauper societies, are yokes to the neck. We pain ourselves to please nobody. There are natural ways of arriving at the same ends at which these aim, but do not arrive. Why

should all virtue work in one and the same way?"
. . . "And why drag this dead weight of a Sunday-school over the whole of Christendom? It is natural and beautiful that childhood should inquire, and maturity should teach; but it is time enough to answer questions when they are asked. Do not shut up the young people against their will in a pew, and force the children to ask them questions for an hour against their will."

Now, without agreeing with him in all points, we may sympathise with him.

Ellesmere. I agree with him.

Dunsford. I knew you would. You love an extreme.

Milverton. But look now. It is well to say, "It is natural and beautiful that the young should ask and the old should teach"; but then the old should be capable of teaching, which is not the case we have to deal with. Institutions are often only to meet individual failings. Let there be more instructed elders, and the "dead weight" of Sunday-schools would be less needed.

I think the result of our thoughts would be, that there should be as much life, joy, and Nature put into teaching as can be; but I, for one, am not prepared to say that the most mechanical process is not better than none.

Ellesmere. Well, you have now shut up the subject, according to your fashion, in a rounded sentence; and you think after that there is nothing more to be said. But I say it goes to my heart——

Dunsford. What is that?

Ellesmere. To my heart to see the unmerciful quantity of instruction that little children go through on a Sunday. I suppose I am a very wicked man; but I know how wearied I should have been, at any time of my life, if so much virtuous precept and good doctrine had been poured into me.

Milverton. Well, I will not fight certainly for anything that is to make Sunday a wearisome day for children. Indeed, what I meant by putting more joy and life into teaching was, that in such a thing as this Sunday-schooling, for instance, a judicious man, far from being anxious to get a certain quantity of routine done about it, would do with the least—would endeavour to connect it with something interesting—would, in a word, love children, and not Sunday-schools.

Ellesmere. Ah, we will have no more about Sunday-schools. I know we all agree in reality, although Dunsford has been looking very grave and has not said a word. I wanted to tell you that I think you are quite right, Milverton, in saying a good deal about multifariousness of pursuit. You see a wretch of a pedant who knows all about tetrameters or statutes of uses, but who, as you hinted an essay or two ago, can hardly answer his child a question as they walk about the garden together. The man has never given a good thought or look to Nature. Well then, again, what a stupid thing it is that we are not all taught music. Why learn the language of many portions of mankind, and leave the universal language of the feelings, as you would call it, unlearnt?

Milverton. I quite agree with you; but I thought you always set your face, or rather your ears, against music.

Dunsford. So did I.

Ellesmere. I should like to know all about it. It is not to my mind that a cultivated man should be quite thrown out by any topic of conversation, or that there should be any form of human endeavour or accomplishment which he has no conception of.

Dunsford. I liked what you said, Milverton, about the philosophy of making light of many things, and the way of looking at life that may thus be given to those we educate. I rather doubted at first, though, whether you were not going to assign too much power to education in the modification of temper. But, certainly, the mode of looking at the daily events of life, little or great, and the consequent habits of captiousness or magnanimity, are just the matters which the young especially imitate their elders in.

Milverton. You see, the very worst kind of tempers are established upon the fretting care for trifles that I want to make war upon in the essay. A man is choleric. Well, it is a very bad thing; it tends to frighten those about him into falseness. He has outrageous bursts of temper. He is humble for days afterwards. His dependants rather like him after all. They know that "his bark is worse than his bite." Then there is your gloomy man, often a man who punishes himself most—perhaps a large-hearted, humorous, but sad man, at the same time liveable with. He does not care for trifles. But it is your acid-sensitive (I must join words like Mirabeau's Grandison-Cromwell, to get what I mean), and your cold, querulous people that need to have angels to live with them. Now education has often had a great deal to do with the making of these choice tempers. They are somewhat artificial productions. And they are the worst.

Dunsford. You know a saying attributed to the Bishop of —— about temper. No? Somebody, I suppose, was excusing something on the score of temper, to which the Bishop replied, "Temper is nine-tenths of Christianity."

Milverton. There is an appearance we see in Nature, not far from here, by the way, that has often put me in mind of the effect of temper upon men. It is in the lowlands near the sea, where, when the tide is not up (the man out of temper), there is a slimy, patchy, diseased-looking surface of mud and sick seaweed. You pass by in a few hours, there is a beautiful lake, water up to the green grass (the man in temper again), and the whole landscape brilliant with reflected light.

Ellesmere. And to complete the likeness, the good temper and the full tide last about the same time—with some men at least. It is so like you, Milverton, to have that simile in your mind. There is nothing you see in Nature, but you must instantly find a parallel for it in man. Sermons in stones you will not see, else I am sure you might. Here is a good hard flint for you to see your next essay in.

Milverton. It will do very well, as my next will be on the subject of population.

Ellesmere. What day are we to have it? I think I have a particular engagement for that day.

Milverton. I must come upon you unawares.

Ellesmere. After the essay you certainly might. Let us decamp now and do something great in the way of education—teach Rollo, though he is but a short-haired dog, to go into the water. That will be a feat.

CHAPTER IX.

ELLESMERE succeeded in persuading Rollo to go into the water, which proved more, he said, than the whole of Milverton's essay, how much might be done by judicious education. Before leaving my friends, I promised to come over again to Worth-Ashton in a day or two, to hear another essay. I came early and found them reading their letters.

" You remember Annesleigh at college," said Milverton, " do you not, Dunsford ? "

Dunsford. Yes.

Milverton. Here is a long letter from him. He is evidently vexed at the newspaper articles about his conduct in a matter of ——, and he writes to tell me that he is totally misrepresented.

Dunsford. Why does he not explain this publicly ?

Milverton. Yes, you naturally think so at first, but such a mode of proceeding would never do for a man in office, and rarely, perhaps, for any man. At least, so the most judicious people seem to think. I have known a man in office bear patiently, without attempting any answer, a serious charge which a few lines would have entirely answered, indeed, turned the other way. But then he thought, I imagine, that if you once begin answering, there is no end to it, and also, which is more important, that the public journals were not a tribunal which he was called to appear before. He had his official superiors.

Dunsford. It should be widely known and acknowledged then, that silence does not give consent in these cases.

Milverton. It is known, though not, perhaps, sufficiently.

Dunsford. What a fearful power this anonymous journalism is!

Milverton. There is a great deal certainly that is mischievous in it; but take it altogether, it is a wonderful product of civilisation—morally too. Even as regards those qualities which would in general, to use a phrase of Bacon's, "be noted as deficients" in the press, in courtesy and forbearance, for example, it makes a much better figure than might have been expected; as any one would testify, I suspect, who had observed, or himself experienced, the temptations incident to writing on short notice, without much opportunity of after-thought or correction, upon subjects about which he had already expressed an opinion.

Dunsford. Is the anonymousness absolutely necessary?

Milverton. I have often thought whether it is. If the anonymousness were taken away, the press would lose much of its power; but then, why should it not lose a portion of its power, if that portion is only built upon some delusion?

Ellesmere. It is a question of expediency. As government of all kinds becomes better managed, there is less necessity for protection for the press. It must be recollected, however, that this anonymousness (to coin a word) may not only be useful to protect us from any abuse of power, but that at least it takes away that temptation to discuss things in an insufficient manner which arises from personal fear of giving offence. Then, again, there is an advantage in considering arguments without reference to persons. If well-known authors wrote for the press and gave their signatures, we should often pass by the arguments unfairly, saying, "Oh, it is only so-and-so: that is the way he always looks at things," without seeing whether it is the right way for the occasion in question.

Milverton. But take the other side, Ellesmere. What national dislikes are fostered by newspaper articles, and——

Ellesmere. Articles in reviews and by books.

Milverton. Yes, but somehow or other, people imagine that newspapers speak the opinion of a much greater number of people——

Ellesmere. Do not let us talk any more about it. We may become wise enough and well-managed enough to do without this anonymousness: we may not. How it would astound an ardent Whig or Radical of the last generation if we could hear such a sentiment as this—as a toast we will say—" The Press: and may we become so civilised as to be able to take away some of its liberty."

Milverton. It may be put another way : "May it become so civilised that we shall not want to take away any of its liberty." But I see you are tired of this subject. Shall we go on the lawn and have our essay ?

We assented, and Milverton read the following :—

UNREASONABLE CLAIMS IN SOCIAL AFFEC- TIONS AND RELATIONS.

We are all apt to magnify the importance of what-ever we are thinking about, which is not to be won-dered at ; for everything human has an outlet into infinity, which we come to perceive on considering it. But with a knowledge of this tendency, I still venture to say that, of all that concerns mankind, this subject has, perhaps, been the least treated of in regard to its significance. For once that unreasonable expectations of gratitude have been reproved, ingratitude has been denounced a thousand times ; and the same may be said of inconstancy, unkindness in friendship, neglected merit and the like.

To begin with ingratitude. Human beings seldom have the demands upon each other which they imagine ; and for what they have done they frequently ask an impossible return. Moreover, when people really have done others a service, the persons benefited often do not understand it. Could they have understood it, the benefactor, perhaps, would not have had to perform it.

You cannot expect gratitude from them in proportion
to your enlightenment.   Then, again, where the service
is a palpable one, thoroughly understood, we often
require that the gratitude for it should bear down all
the rest of the man's character.   The dog is the very
emblem of faithfulness; yet I believe it is found that
he will sometimes like the person who takes him out
and amuses him more than the person who feeds him.
So, amongst bipeds, the most solid service must sometimes give way to the claims of congeniality.   Human
creatures are, happily, not to be swayed by self-interest
alone : they are many-sided creatures ; there are num-
berless modes of attaching their affections.   Not only
like likes like, but unlike likes unlike.

To give an instance which must often occur.   Two
persons, both of feeble will, act together : one as
superior, the other as inferior.   The superior is very
kind; the inferior is grateful.   Circumstances occur
to break this relation.   The inferior comes under a
superior of strong will, who is not, however, as tolerant
and patient as his predecessor.   But this second
superior soon acquires unbounded influence over the
inferior : if the first one looks on, he may wonder at
the alacrity and affection of his former subordinate
towards the new man, and talk much about ingratitude.
But the inferior has now found somebody to lean upon
and to reverence.   And he cannot deny his nature and
be otherwise than he is.   In this case it does not look
like ingratitude, except perhaps to the complaining
person.   But there are doubtless numerous instances
in which, if we saw all the facts clearly, we should no

more confirm the charge of ingratitude than we do here.

Then, again, we seldom make sufficient allowance for the burden which there is in obligation, at least to all but great and good minds. There are some people who can receive as heartily as they would give; but the obligation of an ordinary person to an ordinary person is more apt to be brought to mind as a present sore than as a past delight.

Amongst the unreasonable views of the affections, the most absurd one has been the fancy that love entirely depends upon the will; still more that the love of others for us is to be guided by the inducements which seem probable to us. We have served them; we think only of them; we are their lovers, or fathers, or brothers: we deserve and require to be loved and to have the love proved to us. But love is not like property: it has neither duties nor rights. You argue for it in vain; and there is no one who can give it you. It is not his or hers to give. Millions of bribes and infinite arguments cannot prevail. For it is not a substance, but a relation. There is no royal road. We are loved as we are lovable to the person loving. It is no answer to say that in some cases the love is based on no reality, but is solely in the imagination—that is, that we are loved not for what we are, but for what we are fancied to be. That will not bring it any more into the dominions of logic; and love still remains the same untamable creature, deaf to advocacy, blind to other people's idea of merit, and not a substance to be weighed or numbered at all.

Then, as to the complaints about broken friendship. Friendship is often outgrown; and his former child's clothes will no more fit a man than some of his former friendships. Often a breach of friendship is supposed to occur when there is nothing of the kind. People see one another seldom; their courses in life are different; they meet, and their intercourse is constrained. They fancy that their friendship is mightily cooled. But imagine the dearest friends, one coming home after a long sojourn, the other going out to new lands: the ships that carry these meet: the friends talk together in a confused way not relevant at all to their friendship, and, if not well assured of their mutual regard, might naturally fancy that it was much abated. Something like this occurs daily in the stream of the world. Then, too, unless people are very unreasonable, they cannot expect that their friends will pass into new systems of thought and action without new ties of all kinds being created, and some modification of the old ones taking place.

When we are talking of exorbitant claims made for the regard of others, we must not omit those of what is called neglected merit. A man feels that he has abilities or talents of a particular kind, that he has shown them, and still he is a neglected man. I am far from saying that merit is sufficiently looked out for: but a man may take the sting out of any neglect of his merits by thinking that at least it does not arise from malice prepense, as he almost imagines in his anger. Neither the public, nor individuals, have the time, or

will, resolutely to neglect anybody. What pleases us
we admire and further: if a man in any profession,
calling, or art, does things which are beyond us, we
are as guiltless of neglecting him as the Caffres are of
neglecting the differential calculus. Milton sells his
"Paradise Lost" for ten pounds; there is no record of
Shakespeare dining much with Queen Elizabeth. And
it is Utopian to imagine that statues will be set up to
right men in their day.

The same arguments which applied to the complaints
of ingratitude, apply to the complaints of neglected
merit. The merit is oftentimes not understood. Be it
ever so manifest, it cannot absorb men's attention.
When it is really great, it has not been brought out by
the hope of reward, any more than the kindest services
by the hope of gratitude. In neither case is it becoming
or rational to be clamorous about payment.

There is one thing that people hardly ever remember,
or, indeed, have imagination enough to conceive;
namely, the effect of each man being shut up in his
individuality. Take a long course of sayings and
doings in which many persons have been engaged.
Each one of them is in his own mind the centre of the
web, though, perhaps, he is at the edge of it. We know
that in our observations of the things of sense, any
difference in the points from which the observation is
taken gives a different view of the same thing. Moreover, in the world of sense, the objects and the points
of view are each indifferent to the rest; but in life the
points of views are centres of action that have had
something to do with the making of the things looked

at. If we could calculate the moral parallax arising from these causes, we should see, by the mere aid of the intellect, how unjust we often are in our complaints of ingratitude, inconstancy, and neglect. But without these nice calculations, such errors of view may be corrected at once by humility, a more sure method than the most enlightened appreciation of the cause of error. Humility is the true cure for many a needless heartache.

It must not be supposed that in thus opposing unreasonable views of social affections, anything is done to dissever such affections. The Duke of Wellington, writing to a man in a dubious position of authority, says "The less you claim, the more you will have." This is remarkably true of the affections; and there is scarcely anything that would make men happier than teaching them to watch against unreasonableness in their claims of regard and affection; and which at the same time would be more likely to ensure their getting what may be their due.

———————

Ellesmere (clapping his hands). An essay after my heart : worth tons of soft trash. In general you are amplifying duties, telling everybody that they are to be so good to every other body. Now it is as well to let every other body know that he is not to expect all he may fancy from everybody. A man complains that his prosperous friends neglect him : infinitely overrating, in all probability, his claims, and his friends' power of doing anything for him. Well, then, you may think me very hard, but I say that the most absurd claims are often put forth on the ground of relationship.

I do not deny that there is something in blood, but it must not be made too much of. Near relations have great opportunities of attaching each other; if they fail to use these, I do not think it is well to let them imagine that mere relationship is to be the talisman of affection.

Dunsford. I do not see exactly how to answer all that you or Milverton have said; but I am not prepared, as official people say, to agree with you. I especially disagree with what Milverton has said about love. He leaves much too little power to the will.

Milverton. I daresay I may have done so. These are very deep matters, and any one view about them does not exhaust them. I remember C—— once saying to me that a man never utters anything without error. He may even think of it rightly; but he cannot bring it out rightly. It turns a little false, as it were, when it quits the brain and comes into life.

Ellesmere. I thought you would soon go over to the soft side. Here, Rollo; there's a good dog. You do not form unreasonable expectations, do you? A very little petting puts you into an ecstasy, and you are much wiser than many a biped who is full of his claims for gratitude, and friendship, and love, and who is always longing for well-merited rewards to fall into his mouth. Down, dog!

Milverton. Poor animal! it little knows that all this sudden notice is only by way of ridiculing us. Why I did not maintain my ground stoutly against Dunsford is, that I am always afraid of pushing moral conclusions too far. Since we have been talking, I think I see

more clearly than I did before what I mean to convey
by the essay—namely, that men fall into unreasonable
views respecting the affections *from imagining that the
general laws of the mind are suspended for the sake of
the affections.*

Dunsford. That seems safer ground.

Milverton. Now to illustrate what I mean by a very
similar instance. The mind is avid of new impressions.
It " travels over," or thinks it travels over, another
mind ; and, though it may conceal its wish for " fresh
fields and pastures new," it does so wish. However
harsh, therefore, and unromantic it may seem, the best
plan is to humour Nature, and not to exhaust by over-
frequent presence the affection of those whom we would
love, or whom we would have to love us. I would not
say, after the manner of Rochefoucauld, that the less
we see of people the more we like them ; but there are
certain limits of sociality ; and prudent reserve and
absence may find a place in the management of the
tenderest relations.

Dunsford. Yes, all this is true enough : I do not see
anything hard in this. But then there is the other
side. Custom is a great aid to affection.

Milverton. Yes. All I say is, do not fancy that the
general laws are suspended for the sake of any one
affection.

Dunsford. Still this does not go to the question
whether there is not something more of will in affection
than you make out. You would speak of inducements and counter-inducements, aids and hindrances ;
but I cannot but think you are limiting the power of

will, and therefore limiting duty. Such views tend to make people easily discontented with each other, and prevent their making efforts to get over offences, and to find out what is lovable in those about them.

Ellesmere. Here we are in the deep places again. I see you are pondering, Milverton. It is a question, as a minister would say when Parliament perplexes him, that we must go to the country upon; each man's heart will, perhaps, tell him best about it. For my own part, I think that the continuance of affection, as the rise of it, depends more on the taste being satisfied, or at least not disgusted, than upon any other single thing. Our hearts may be touched at our being loved by people essentially distasteful to us, whose modes of talking and acting are a continual offence to us ; but whether we can love them in return is a question.

Milverton. Yes, we can, I think. I begin to see that it is a question of degree. The word love includes many shades of meaning. When it includes admiration, of course we cannot be said to love those in whom we see nothing to admire. But this seldom happens in the mixed characters of real life. The upshot of it all seems to me to be, that, as Guizot says of civilisation, every impulse has room ; so in the affections, every inducement and counter-inducement has its influence ; and the result is not a simple one, which can be spoken of as if it were alike on all occasions and with all men.

Dunsford. I am still unanswered, I think, Milverton. What you say is still wholly built upon inducements, and does not touch the power of will.

Milverton. No ; it does not.

Ellesmere. We must leave that alone. Infinite piles of books have not as yet lifted us up to a clear view of that matter.

Dunsford. Well, then, we must leave it as a vexed question ; but let it be seen that there is such a question. Now, as to another thing; you speak, Milverton, of men's not making allowance enough for the unpleasant weight of obligation. I think that weight seems to have increased in modern times. Essex could give Bacon a small estate, and Bacon could take it comfortably, I have no doubt. That is a much more wholesome state of things among friends than the present.

Milverton. Yes, undoubtedly. An extreme notion about independence has made men much less generous in receiving.

Dunsford. It is a falling off, then. There was another comment I had to make. I think, when you speak about the exorbitant demands of neglected merit, you should say more upon the neglect of the just demands of merit.

Milverton. I would have the Government and the public in general try by all means to understand and reward merit, especially in those matters wherein excellence cannot, otherwise, meet with large present reward. But, to say the truth, I would have this done, not with the view of fostering genius so much as of fulfilling duty : I would say to a minister—it is becoming in you—it is well for the nation, to reward, as far as you can, and dignify, men of genius. Whether you will do them any good, or bring forth more of them, I do not know.

Ellesmere. Men of great genius are often such a sensitive race, so apt to be miserable in many other than pecuniary ways and want of public estimation, that I am not sure that distress and neglect do not take their minds off worse discomforts. It is a kind of grievance, too, that they like to have.

Dunsford. Really, Ellesmere, that is a most unfeeling speech.

Milverton. At any rate, it is right for us to honour and serve a great man. It is our nature to do so, if we are worth anything. We may put aside the question whether our honour will do him more good than our neglect. That is a question for him to look to. The world has not yet so largely honoured deserving men in their own time, that we can exactly pronounce what effect it would have upon them.

Ellesmere. Come, Rollo, let us leave these men of sentiment. Oh, you will not go, as your master does not move. Look how he wags his tail, and almost says, " I should dearly like to have a hunt after the water-rat we saw in the pond the other day, but master is talking philosophy, and requires an intelligent audience." These dogs are dear creatures, it must be owned. Come, Milverton, let us have a walk.

CHAPTER X.

AFTER the reading in the last chapter, my friends walked homewards with me as far as Durley Wood, which is about half-way between Worth-Ashton and my

house.   As we rested here, we bethought ourselves that
it would be a pleasant spot for us to come to sometimes
and read our essays.   So we agreed to name a day
for meeting there.   The day was favourable, we met as
we had appointed, and finding some beech logs lying
very opportunely, took possession of them for our
council.   We seated Ellesmere on one that we called
the woolsack, but which he said he felt himself unworthy
to occupy in the presence of King Log, pointing to
mine.   These nice points of etiquette being at last
settled, Milverton drew out his papers and was about
to begin reading, when Ellesmere thus interrupted
him :—

Ellesmere. You were not in earnest, Milverton, about
giving us an essay on population ?   Because if so, I
think I shall leave this place to you and Dunsford and
the ants.

Milverton. I certainly have been meditating something of the sort ; but have not been able to make much
of it.

Ellesmere. If I had been living in those days when
it first beamed upon mankind that the earth was round,
I am sure I should have said, " We know now the
bounds of the earth : there are no interminable plains
joined to the regions of the sun, allowing of indefinite
sketchy outlines at the edges of maps.   That little
creature man will immediately begin to think that his
world is too small for him."

Milverton. There has probably been as much folly
uttered by political economy as against it, which is
saying something.   The danger as regards theories of

political economy is the obvious one of their abstract conclusions being applied to concrete things.

Ellesmere. As if we were to expect mathematical lines to bear weights.

Milverton. Something like that. With a good system of logic pervading the public mind, this danger would of course be avoided; but such a state of mind is not likely to occur in any public that we or our grandchildren are likely to have to deal with. As it is, an ordinary man hears some conclusion of political economy, showing some particular tendency of things, which in real life meets with many counteractions of all kinds: but he, perhaps, adopts the conclusion without the least abatement, and would work it into life, as if all went on there like a rule-of-three sum.

Ellesmere. After all, this error arises from the man's not having enough political economy. It is not that a theory is good on paper, but unsound in real life. It is only that in real life you cannot get at the simple state of things to which the theory would rightly apply. You want many other theories and the just composition of them all to be able to work the whole problem. That being done (which, however, scarcely can be done), the result on paper might be read off as applicable at once to life. But now, touching the essay; since we are not to have population, what is it to be?

Milverton. Public improvements.

Ellesmere. Nearly as bad; but as this is a favourite subject of yours, I suppose it will not be polite to go away.

Milverton. No; you must listen.

PUBLIC IMPROVEMENTS.

What are possessions ? To an individual, the stores
of his own heart and mind pre-eminently. His truth
and valour are amongst the first. His contentedness,
or his resignation may be put next. Then his sense of
beauty, surely a possession of great moment to him.
Then all those mixed possessions which result from
the social affections—great possessions, unspeakable
delights, much greater than the gift last mentioned in
the former class, but held on more uncertain tenure.
Lastly, what are generally called possessions? However often we have heard of the vanity, uncertainty,
and vexation that beset these last, we must not let this
repetition deaden our minds to the fact.

Now, national possessions must be estimated by the
same gradation that we have applied to individual
possessions. If we consider national luxury, we shall
see how small a part it may add to national happiness.
Men of deserved renown, and peerless women, lived
upon what we should now call the coarsest fare, and
paced the rushes in their rooms with as high, or as contented thoughts, as their better-fed and better-clothed
descendants can boast of. Man is limited in this
direction; I mean, in the things that concern his
personal gratification ; but when you come to the higher
enjoyments, the expansive power both in him and them
is greater. As Keats says,

> " A thing of beauty is a joy for ever;
>   Its loveliness increases; it will never
>   Pass into nothingness; but still will keep

A bower quiet for us, and a sleep
Full of sweet dreams, and health, and quiet breathing."

What then are a nation's possessions? The great words that have been said in it; the great deeds that have been done in it; the great buildings, and the great works of art, that have been made in it. A man says a noble saying: it is a possession, first to his own race, then to mankind. A people get a noble building built for them: it is an honour to them, also a daily delight and instruction. It perishes. The remembrance of it is still a possession. If it was indeed pre-eminent, there will be more pleasure in thinking of it than in being with others of inferior order and design.

On the other hand, a thing of ugliness is potent for evil. It deforms the taste of the thoughtless: it frets the man who knows how bad it is: it is a disgrace to the nation who raised it; an example and an occasion for more monstrosities. If it is a great building in a great city, thousands of people pass it daily, and are the worse for it, or at least not the better. It must be done away with. Next to the folly of doing a bad thing is that of fearing to undo it. We must not look at what it has cost, but at what it is. Millions may be spent upon some foolish device which will not the more make it into a possession, but only a more noticeable detriment.

It must not be supposed that works of art are the only, or the chief, public improvements needed in any country. Wherever men congregate, the elements become scarce. The supply of air, light, and water is then a matter of the highest public importance: and the magnificent utilitarianism of the Romans should precede the nice sense of beauty of the Greeks. Or rather, the former should be worked out in the latter. Sanitary improvements, like most good works, may be made to fulfil many of the best human objects. Charity, social order, conveniency of living, and the love of the beautiful, may all be furthered by such improvements. A people is seldom so well employed as when, not suffering their attention to be absorbed by foreign quarrels and domestic broils, they bethink themselves of winning back those blessing of Nature which assemblages of men mostly vitiate, exclude, or destroy.

Public improvements are sometimes most difficult in free countries. The origination of them is difficult there, many diverse minds having to be persuaded. The individual, or class, resistance to the public good is harder to conquer than in despotic states. And, what is most embarrassing, perhaps, individual progress in the same direction, or individual doings in some other way, form a great hindrance, sometimes, to public enterprise. On the other hand, the energy of a free people is a mine of public welfare; and individual effort brings many good things to bear in much shorter time than any government could be expected to move in. A judicious statesman considers these things; and sets himself especially to overcome those peculiar obstacles to public improvement which belong to the institutions of his country. Adventure in a despotic state, combined action in a free state, are the objects which peculiarly demand his attention.

To return to works of art. In this also the genius of the people is to be heeded. There may have been, there may be, nations requiring to be diverted from the love of art to stern labour and industrial conquests. But certainly it is not so with the Anglo-Saxon race, or with the Northern races generally. Money may enslave them; logic may enslave them; art never will. The chief men, therefore, in these races will do well sometimes to contend against the popular current, and to convince their people that there are other sources of delight, and other objects worthy of human endeavour, than severe money-getting or mere material successes of any kind.

In fine, the substantial improvement, and even the embellishment of towns, is a work which both the central and local governing bodies in a country should keep a steady hand upon. It especially concerns them. What are they there for but to do that which individuals cannot do? It concerns them, too, as it tells upon the health, morals, education, and refined pleasures of the people they govern. In doing it, they should avoid pedantry, parsimony, and favouritism; and their mode of action should be large, considerate, and foreseeing. Large; inasmuch as they must not easily be contented with the second best in any of their projects. Considerate; inasmuch as they have to think what their people need most, not what will make most show. And therefore, they should be contented, for instance, at their work going on underground for a

time, or in byways, if needful; the best charity in
public works, as in private, being often that which
courts least notice.   Lastly, their work should be with
foresight, recollecting that cities grow up about us like
young people, before we are aware of it.

Ellesmere. Another very merciful essay!   When we
had once got upon the subject of sanitary improvements, I thought we should soon be five fathom deep in
blue-books, reports, interminable questions of sewerage,
and horrors of all kinds.

Milverton. I am glad you own that I have been very
tender of your impatience in this essay.   People, I
trust, are now so fully aware of the immense importance of sanitary improvements, that we do not want
the elementary talking about such things that was
formerly necessary.   It is difficult, though, to say too
much about sanitary matters, that is, if by saying much
one could gain attention.   I am convinced that the
most fruitful source of physical evil to mankind has
been impure air, arising from circumstances which
might have been obviated.   Plagues and pestilences of
all kinds, cretinism too, and all scrofulous disorders,
are probably mere questions of ventilation.   A district
may require ventilation as well as a house.

Ellesmere. Seriously speaking, I quite agree with
you.   And what delights me in sanitary improvements
is, that they can hardly do harm.   Give a poor man
good air, and you do not diminish his self-reliance.
You only add to his health and vigour—make more of
a man of him.   But now that the public mind, as it is

facetiously called, has got hold of the idea of these improvements, everybody will be chattering about them.

Milverton. The very time when those who really do care for these matters should be watchful to make the most of the tide in their favour, and should not suffer themselves to relax their efforts because there is no originality now about such things.

Dunsford. Custom soon melts off the wings which Novelty alone has lent to Benevolence.

Ellesmere. And down comes the charitable Icarus. A very good simile, my dear Dunsford, but rather of the Latin-verse order. I almost see it worked into an hexameter and pentameter, and delighting the heart of an Eton boy.

Dunsford. Ellesmere is more than usually vicious to-day, Milverton. A great "public improvement" would be to clip the tongues of some of these lawyers.

Ellesmere. Possibly. I have just been looking again at that part of the essay, Milverton, where you talk of the little gained by national luxury. I think with you. There is an immensity of nonsense uttered about making people happy, which is to be done, according to happiness-mongers, by quantities of sugar and tea, and such-like things. One knows the importance of food, but there is no Elysium to be got out of it.

Milverton. I know what you mean. There is a kind of pity for the people now in vogue which is most effeminate. It is a sugared sort of Robespierre talk about "The poor but virtuous People." To address such stuff to the people is not to give them anything, but to take away what they have. Suppose you could give them oceans of tea and mountains of sugar, and abundance of any luxury that you choose to imagine, but at the same time you inserted a hungry, envious spirit in them, what have you done? Then, again, this envious spirit, when it is turned to difference of station, what good can it do? Can you give station according to merit? Is life long enough for it?

Ellesmere. Of course we cannot always be weighing men with nicety, and saying, "Here is your place, here yours."

Milverton. Then, again, what happiness do you confer on men by teaching them to disrespect their superiors in rank, by turning all the embellishments which adorn various stations wrong side out, putting everything in its lowest form, and then saying, "What do you see to admire here?" You do not know what injury you may do a man when you destroy all reverence in him. It will be found out some day that men derive more pleasure and profit from having superiors than from having inferiors.

Dunsford. It is seldom that I bring you back to your subject, but we are really a long way off at present; and I want to know, Milverton, what you would do specifically in the way of public improvements. Of course you cannot say in an essay what you would do in such matters, but amongst ourselves. In London, for instance.

Milverton. The first thing for Government to do, Dunsford, in London, or any other great town, is to secure open spaces in it and about it. Trafalgar

Square may be dotted with hideous absurdities, but it is an open space. They may collect together there specimens of every variety of meanness and bad taste; but they cannot prevent its being a better thing than if it were covered with houses. Public money is scarcely ever so well employed as in securing bits of waste ground and keeping them as open spaces. Then, as under the most favourable circumstances, we are likely to have too much carbon in the air of any town, we should plant trees to restore the just proportions of the air as far as we can.* Trees are also what the heart and the eye desire most in towns. The Boulevards in Paris show the excellent effect of trees against buildings. There are many parts of London where rows of trees might be planted along the streets. The weighty dulness of Portland Place, for instance, might be thus relieved. Of course, in any scheme of public improvements, the getting rid of smoke is one of the first objects.

Ellesmere. Yes, smoke is a great abuse; but then there is something ludicrous about it, just as there is about sewerage. I believe, myself, that for one person that the Corn Laws have injured, a dozen have had their lives shortened and their happiness abridged in every way by these less palpable nuisances. But there is no grandeur in opposing them—no "good cry" to be raised. And so, as abuses cannot be met in our days but by agitation—a committee, secretaries, clerks, newspapers, and a review—and as agitation in this case holds out fewer inducements than usual, we have

* See "Health of Towns Report," 1844, vol. i., p. 44.

gone on year after year being poisoned by these various nuisances, at an incalculable expense of life and money.

Milverton. There is something in what you say, I think, but you press it too far; for of late these sanitary subjects have worked themselves into notice, as you yourself admit.

Ellesmere. Late indeed.

Milverton. Well, but to go on with schemes for improving London. Open spaces, trees—then comes the supply of water. This is one of the first things to be done. Philadelphia has given an example which all towns ought to imitate. It is a matter requiring great thought, and the various plans should be thoroughly canvassed before the choice is made. Great beauty and the highest utility may be combined in supplying a town like London with water. By the way, how much water do you think London requires daily?

Ellesmere. As much as the Serpentine and the water in St. James's Park.

Milverton. You are not so far out.

Well, then, having gone through the largest things that must be attended to, we come to minor matters. It is a great pity that the system of building upon leases should be so commonly adopted. Nobody expects to live out the leasehold term which he takes to build upon. But things would be better done if people were more averse to having anything to do with leasehold property. C. always says that the modern lath-and-plaster system is a wickedness, and upon my word I think he is right. It is inconceivable to me how a man can make up his mind to build, or to do anything else, in a temporary, slight, insincere fashion. What has a man to say for himself who must sum up the doings of his life in this way, "I chiefly employed myself in making or selling things which seemed to be good and were not, and nobody has occasion to bless me for anything I have done."

Ellesmere. Humph! you put it mildly. But the man has made perhaps seven per cent. off his money; or, if he has made no per cent., has ruined several men of his own trade, which is not to go for nothing when a man is taking stock of his good deeds.

Milverton. There is one thing I forgot to say, that we want more individual will in building, I think. As it is at present, a great builder takes a plot of ground and turns out innumerable houses, all alike, the same faults and merits running through each, thus adding to the general dulness of things.

Ellesmere. Lady Mary Wortley Montagu, when she came from abroad, remarked that all her friends seemed to have got into drawing-rooms which were like a grand piano, first a large square or oblong room, and then a small one. Quite Georgian, this style of architecture. But now I think we are improving immensely—at any rate in the outside of houses. By the way, Milverton, I want to ask you one thing : How is it that Governments and Committees, and the bodies that manage matters of taste, seem to be more tasteless than the average run of people ? I will wager anything that the cabmen round Trafalgar Square would have made a better thing of it than it is. If you had put before them several prints of fountains, they would not have chosen those.

Milverton. I think with you, but I have no theory to account for it. I suppose that these committees are frequently hampered by other considerations than those which come before the public when they are looking at the work done; and this may be some excuse. There was a custom which I have heard prevailed in former days in some of the Italian cities, of making large models of the works of art that were to adorn the city, and putting them up in the places intended for the works when finished, and then inviting criticism. It would really be a very good plan in some cases.

Ellesmere. Now, Milverton, would you not forthwith pull down such things as Buckingham Palace and the National Gallery? Dunsford looks at me as if I were going to pull down the Constitution.

Milverton. I would pull them down to a certainty, or some parts of them at any rate; but whether "forthwith" is another question. There are greater things, perhaps, to be done first. We must consider, too,

> "That eternal want of pence
> Which vexes public men."

Still, I think we ought always to look upon such buildings as temporary arrangements, and they vex one less then. The Palace ought to be in the higher part of the Park, perhaps on that slope opposite Piccadilly.

Dunsford. Well, it does amuse me the way in which you youngsters go on, pulling down, in your industrious imaginations, palaces and national galleries, building aqueducts and cloacæ maximæ, forming parks, destroying smoke (so large a part of every Londoner's diet), and abridging plaster, without fear of Chancellors of the Exchequer, and the resistance of mankind in general.

Milverton. We must begin by thinking boldly about things. That is a larger part of any undertaking than it seems, perhaps.

Dunsford. We must, I am afraid, break off our pleasant employment of projecting public improvements, unless we mean to be dinnerless.

Ellesmere. A frequent fate of great projectors, I fear.

Milverton. Now then, homewards.

CHAPTER XI.

My readers will, perhaps, agree with me in being sorry to find that we are coming to the end of our present series. I say, " my readers," though I have so little part in purveying for them, that I mostly consider myself one of them. It is no light task, however, to give a good account of a conversation ; and I say this, and would wish people to try whether I am not right in saying so, not to call attention to my labour in the matter, but because it may be well to notice how difficult it is to report anything truly. Were this better known, it might be an aid to charity, and prevent some of those feuds which grow out of the poverty of man's power to express, to apprehend, to represent, rather than out of any malignant part of his nature. But I must not go on moralising. I almost feel that Ellesmere is looking over my shoulder, and breaking into my discourse with sharp words, which I have lately been so much accustomed to.

I had expected that we should have many more readings this summer, as I knew that Milverton had prepared more essays for us. But finding, as he said, that the other subjects he had in hand were larger than he had anticipated, or was prepared for, he would not read even to *us* what he had written. Though I was very sorry for this—for I may not be the chronicler in another year—I could not but say he was right. Indeed, my ideas of literature, nourished as they have been in much solitude, and by the reading, if I may say so, mainly of our classical authors, are very high placed, though I hope not fantastical. And, therefore, I would not discourage anyone in expending whatever thought and labour might be in him upon any literary work.

In fine, then, I did not attempt to dissuade Milverton from his purpose of postponing our readings : and we agreed that there should only be one more for the present. I wished it to be at our favourite place on the lawn, which had become endeared to me as the spot of many of our friendly councils.

It was later than usual when I came over to Worth-Ashton for this reading ; and as I gained the brow of the hill, some few clouds tinged with red were just grouping together to form the accustomed pomp upon the exit of the setting sun. I believe I mentioned in the introduction to our first conversation that the ruins of an old castle could be seen from our place of meeting. Milverton and Ellesmere were talking about it as I joined them.

Milverton. Yes, Ellesmere, many a man has looked out of those windows upon a sunset like this, with some of the thoughts that must come into the minds of all men on seeing this great emblem, the setting sun—has felt, in looking at it, his coming end, or the closing of his greatness. Those old walls must have been witness to every kind of human emotion. Henry the Second was there; John, I think; Margaret of Anjou and Cardinal Beaufort; William of Wykeham; Henry the Eighth's Cromwell; and many others who have made some stir in the world.

Ellesmere. And, perhaps, the greatest there were those who made no stir.

"The world knows nothing of its greatest men."

Milverton. I am slow to believe that. I cannot well reconcile myself to the idea that great capacities are given for nothing. They bud out in some way or other.

Ellesmere. Yes, but it may not be in a noisy way.

Milverton. There is one thing that always strikes me very much in looking at the lives of men : how soon, as it were, their course seems to be determined. They say, or do, or think, something which gives a bias at once to the whole of their career.

Dunsford. You may go farther back than that, and speak of the impulses they got from their ancestors.

Ellesmere. Or the nets around them of other people's

ways and wishes. There are many things, you see, that go to make men puppets.

Milverton. I was only noticing the circumstance that there was such a thing, as it appeared to me, as this early direction. But, if it has been ever so unfortunate, a man's folding his hands over it in a melancholy mood, and suffering himself to be made a puppet by it, is a sadly weak proceeding. Most thoughtful men have probably some dark fountains in their souls, by the side of which, if there were time, and it were decorous, they could let their thoughts sit down and wail indefinitely. That long Byron wail fascinated men for a time; because there is that in Human Nature. Luckily, a great deal besides.

Ellesmere. I delight in the helpful and hopeful men.

Milverton. A man that I admire very much, and have met with occasionally, is one who is always of use in any matter he is mixed up with, simply because he wishes that the best should be got out of the thing that is possible. There does not seem much in the description of such a character; but only see it in contrast with that of a brilliant man, for instance, who does not ever fully care about the matter in hand.

Dunsford. I can thoroughly imagine the difference.

Milverton. The human race may be bound up together in some mysterious way, each of us having a profound interest in the fortunes of the whole, and so, to some extent, of every portion of it. Such a man as I have described acts as though he had an intuitive perception of that relation, and therefore a sort of family feeling for mankind, which gives him satisfaction in making the best out of any human affair he has to do with.

But we really must have the essay, and not talk any more. It is on History.

HISTORY.

Among the fathomless things that are about us and within us, is the continuity of time. This gives to life one of its most solemn aspects. We may think to ourselves : Would there could be some halting-place in life, where we could stay, collecting our minds, and see the world drift by us. But no : even while you read this, you are not pausing to read it. As one of the great French preachers, I think, says, We are embarked upon a stream, each in his own little boat, which must move uniformly onwards, till it ceases to move at all. It is a stream that knows " no haste, no rest " ; a boat that knows no haven but one.

This unbated continuity suggests the past as well as the future. We would know what mighty empires this stream of time has flowed through, by what battle-fields it has been tinged, how it has been employed towards fertility, and what beautiful shadows on its surface have been seized by art, or science, or great words, and held in time-lasting, if not in everlasting, beauty. This is what history tells us. Often in a faltering, confused, be-darkened way, like the deed it chronicles. But it is what we have, and we must make the best of it.

The subject of this essay may be thus divided : Why history should be read—how it should be read—by whom it should be written—how it should be written—

and how good writers of history should be called forth, aided, and rewarded.

I. WHY HISTORY SHOULD BE READ.

It takes us out of too much care for the present; it extends our sympathies; it shows us that other men have had their sufferings and their grievances; it enriches discourse, it enlightens travel. So does fiction. But the effect of history is more lasting and suggestive. If we see a place which fiction has treated of, we feel that it has some interest for us ; but show us a spot where remarkable deeds have been done, or remarkable people have lived, and our thoughts cling to it. We employ our own imagination about it : we invent the fiction for ourselves. Again, history is at least the conventional account of things : that which men agree to receive as the right account, and which they discuss as true. To understand their talk, we must know what they are talking about. Again, there is something in history which can seldom be got from the study of the lives of individual men ; namely, the movements of men collectively, and for long periods—of man, in fact, not of men. In history, the composition of the forces that move the world has to be analysed. We must have before us the law of the progress of opinion, the interruptions to it of individual character, the principles on which men act in the main, the trade winds, as we may say, in human affairs, and the recurrent storms which one man's life does not tell us of. Again, by the study of history, we have a chance of becoming tolerant, travelling over the ways of many nations and many

periods ; and we may also acquire that historic tact by
which we collect upon one point of human affairs the
light of many ages.

We may judge of the benefit of historical studies by
observing what great defects are incident to the moral
and political writers who know nothing of history. A
present grievance, or what seems such, swallows up in
their minds all other considerations ; their little bottle
of oil is to still the raging waves of the whole human
ocean ; their system, a thing that the historian has seen
before, perhaps, in many ages, is to reconcile all diversities.   Then they would persuade you that this class of
men is wholly good, that wholly bad ; or that there is
no difference between good and bad.   They may be
shrewd men, considering what they have seen, but
would be much shrewder if they could know how small
a part that is of life.   We may all refer to our boyhood,
and recollect the time when we thought the things about
us were the type of all things everywhere.   That was,
perhaps, after all no silly princess who was for feeding
the famishing people on cakes.   History takes us out
of this confined circle of child-like thought ; and shows
us what are the perennial aims, struggles, and distrac-
tions of mankind.

History has always been set down as the especial
study for statesmen, and for men who take an interest
in public affairs.   For history is to nations what
biography is to individual men.   History is the chart
and compass for national endeavour.   Our early
voyagers are dead : not a plank remains of the old
ships that first essayed unknown waters ; the sea retains

no track; and were it not for the history of these voyages contained in charts, in chronicles, in hoarded lore of all kinds, each voyager, though he were to start with all the aids of advanced civilisation (if you could imagine such a thing without history), would need the boldness of the first voyager.

And so it would be with the statesman, were the civil history of mankind unknown. We live to some extent in peace and comfort upon the results obtained for us by the chronicles of our forefathers. We do not see this without some reflection. But imagine what a full-grown nation would be if it knew no history —like a full-grown man with only a child's experience.

The present is an age of remarkable experiences. Vast improvements have been made in several of the outward things that concern life nearly, from intercourse rapid as lightning to surgical operation without pain. We accept them all; still, the difficulties of government, the management of ourselves, our relations with others, and many of the prime difficulties of life remain but little subdued. History still claims our interest, is still wanted to make us think and act with any breadth of wisdom.

At the same time, however, that we claim for history great powers of instruction, we must not imagine that the examples which it furnishes will enable its readers to anticipate the experience of life. An experienced man reads that Cæsar did this or that, but he says to himself, "I am not Cæsar." Or, indeed, as is most probable, the reader has not to reject the application of the example to himself: for from first to last he sees nothing but experience for Cæsar in what Cæsar was doing. I think it may be observed, too, that general maxims about life gain the ear of the inexperienced, in preference to historical examples. But neither wise sayings nor historical examples can be understood without experience. Words are only symbols. Who can know anything soundly with respect to the complicated affections and struggles of life, unless he has experienced some of them? All knowledge of humanity spreads from within. So in studying history, the lessons it teaches must have something to grow round in the heart they teach. Our own trials, misfortunes, and enterprises are the best lights by which we can read history. Hence it is that many an historian may see far less into the depths of the very history he has himself written than a man who, having acted and suffered, reads the history in question with all the wisdom that comes from action and suffering. Sir Robert Walpole might naturally exclaim, "Do not read history to me, for that, I know, must be false." But if he had read it, I do not doubt that he would have seen through the film of false and insufficient narrative into the depth of the matter narrated, in a way that men of great experience can alone attain to.

II. HOW HISTORY SHOULD BE READ.

I suppose that many who now connect the very word history with the idea of dulness, would have been fond and diligent students of history if it had had fair access to their minds. But they were set down to read histories which were not fitted to be read continuously, or by any but practised students. Some such works are mere framework, a name which the author of the *Statesman* applies to them; very good things, perhaps, for their purpose, but that is not to invite readers to history. You might almost as well read dictionaries with a hope of getting a succinct and clear view of language. When, in any narration, there is a constant heaping up of facts, made about equally significant by the way of telling them, a hasty delineation of characters, and all the incidents moving on as in the fifth act of a confused tragedy, the mind and memory refuse to be so treated; and the reading ends in nothing but a very slight and inaccurate acquaintance with the mere husk of the history. You cannot epitomise the knowledge that it would take years to acquire into a few volumes that may be read in as many weeks.

The most likely way of attracting men's attention to historical subjects will be by presenting them with small portions of history, of great interest, thoroughly examined. This may give them the habit of applying thought and criticism to historical matters.

For, as it is, how are people interested in history? and how do they master its multitudinous assemblage of facts? Mostly, perhaps, in this way. A man cares about some one thing, or person, or event, and plunges into its history, really wishing to master it. This pursuit extends: other points of research are taken up by him at other times. His researches begin to intersect. He finds a connection in things. The texture of his historic acquisitions gradually attains some substance and colour; and so at last he begins to have some dim notions of the myriads of men who came, and saw, and did not conquer—only struggled on as they best might, some of them—and are not.

When we are considering how history should be read, the main thing perhaps is, that the person reading should desire to know what he is reading about, not merely to have read the books that tell of it. The most elaborate and careful historian must omit, or pass lightly over, many points of his subject. He writes for all readers, and cannot indulge private fancies. But history has its particular aspect for each man: there must be portions which he may be expected to dwell upon. And everywhere, even where the history is most laboured, the reader should have something of the spirit of research which was needful for the writer : if only so much as to ponder well the words of the writer. That man reads history, or anything else, at great peril of being thoroughly misled, who has no perception of any truthfulness except that which can be fully ascertained by reference to facts; who does not in the least perceive the truth, or the reverse, of a writer's style, of his epithets, of his reasoning, of his mode of narration. In life, our faith in any narration is much influenced by the personal appearance, voice, and gesture of the person narrating. There is some part of all these things in his writing; and you must look into that well before you can know what faith to give him. One man may make mistakes in names, and dates, and references, and yet have a real substance of truthfulness in him, a wish to enlighten himself and then you. Another may not be wrong in his facts, but have a declamatory or sophistical vein in him, much to be guarded against. A third may be both inaccurate and untruthful, caring not so much for anything as to write his book. And if the reader cares only to read it, sad work they make between them of the memories of former days.

In studying history, it must be borne in mind that a knowledge is necessary of the state of manners, customs, wealth, arts, and science at the different periods treated of. The text of civil history requires a context of this knowledge in the mind of the reader. For the same reason, some of the main facts of the geography of the countries in question should be present to him. If we are ignorant of these aids to history, all history is apt to seem alike to us. It becomes merely a narrative of men of our own time, in our own country; and then we are prone to expect the same views and conduct from them that we do from our contemporaries. It is true that the heroes of antiquity have been represented on the stage in bag-wigs, and the rest of the costume of our grandfathers: but it was the great events of their lives that were thus told—the crisis of their passions—and when we are contemplating the representation of great passions and their consequences, all minor imagery is of little moment. In a long-drawn narrative, however, the more we have in our minds of what concerned the daily life of the people we read about, the better. And in general it may be said that history, like travelling, gives a return in proportion to the knowledge that a man brings to it.

III. BY WHOM HISTORY SHOULD BE WRITTEN.

Before entering directly on this part of the subject, it is desirable to consider a little the difficulties in the way of writing history. We all know the difficulty of getting at the truth of a matter which happened yesterday, and about which we can examine the living actors upon oath. But in history the most significant things may lack the most important part of their evidence. The people who were making history were not thinking of the convenience of future writers of history. Often the historian must contrive to get his insight into matters from evidence of men and things which is like bad pictures of them. The contemporary, if he knew the man, said of the picture, " I should have known it, but it has very little of him in it." The poor historian, with no original before him, has to see through the bad picture into the man. Then, supposing our historian rich in well-selected evidence—I say well-selected, because, as students tell us, for many an historian one authority is of the same weight as another, provided they are both of the same age; still, how difficult is narration even to the man who is rich in well-selected evidence. What a tendency there is to round off a narrative into falsehood; or else by parenthesis to destroy its pith and continuity. Again, the historian knows the end of many of the transactions he narrates. If he did not, how differently often he would narrate them. It would be a most instructive thing to give a man the materials for the account of a great transaction, stopping short of the end, and then

see how different would be his account from the
ordinary ones. Fools have been hardly dealt with in
the saying that the event is their master ("eventus
stultorum magister"), seeing how it rules us all. And
in nothing more than in history. The event is always
present to our minds; along the pathways to it, the
historian and the moralist have walked till they are
beaten pathways, and we imagine that they were so to
the men who first went along them. Indeed, we
almost fancy that these ancestors of ours, looking along
the beaten path, foresaw the event as we do; whereas,
they mostly stumbled upon it suddenly in the forest.
This knowledge of the end we must, therefore, put
down as one of the most dangerous pitfalls which
beset the writers of history. Then consider the difficulty in the "composition," to use an artist's word, of
our historian's picture. Before both the artist and the
historian lies Nature as far as the horizon; how shall
they choose that portion of it which has some unity and
which shall represent the rest? What method is needful in the grouping of facts; what learning, what
patience, what accuracy!

By whom, then, should history be written? In the
first place, by men of some experience in real life; who
have acted and suffered; who have been in crowds, and
seen, perhaps felt, how madly men can care about
nothings; who have observed how much is done in the
world in an uncertain manner, upon sudden impulses and
very little reason; and who, therefore, do not think themselves bound to have a deep-laid theory for all things.
They should be men who have studied the laws of the

affections, who know how much men's opinions depend on the time in which they live, how they vary with their age and their position. To make themselves historians, they should also have considered the combinations amongst men and the laws that govern such things; for there are laws. Moreover our historians, like most men who do great things, must combine in themselves qualities which are held to belong to opposite natures; must at the same time be patient in research and vigorous in imagination, energetic and calm, cautious and enterprising. Such historians, wise, as we may suppose they will be, about the affairs of other men, may, let us hope, be sufficiently wise about their own affairs to understand that no great work can be done without great labour, that no great labour ought to look for its reward. But my readers will exclaim as Rasselas to Imlac on hearing the requisites for a poet, " Enough ! thou hast convinced me that no human being can ever be *an historian*. Proceed with thy narration."

IV. HOW HISTORY SHOULD BE WRITTEN.

One of the first things in writing history is for the historian to recollect that it is history he is writing. The narrative must not be oppressed by reflections, even by wise ones. Least of all should the historian suffer himself to become entangled by a theory or a system. If he does, each fact is taken up by him in a particular way: those facts that cannot be so handled cease to be his facts, and those that offer themselves conveniently are received too fondly by him.

Then, although our historian must not be mastered

by system, he must have some way of taking up his facts and of classifying them. They must not be mere isolated units in his eyes, else he is mobbed by them. And a man in the midst of a crowd, though he may know the names and nature of all the crowd, cannot give an account of their doings. Those who look down from the housetop must do that.

But, above all things, the historian must get out of his own age into the time in which he is writing. Imagination is as much needed for the historian as the poet. You may combine bits of books with other bits of books, and so make some new combinations, and this may be done accurately, and, in general, much of the subordinate preparation for history may be accomplished without any great effort of imagination. But to write history in any large sense of the words, you must be able to comprehend other times. You must know that there is a right and wrong which is not your right and wrong, but yet stands upon the right and wrong of all ages and all hearts. You must also appreciate the outward life and colours of the period you write about. Try to think how the men you are telling of would have spent a day, what were their leading ideas, what they cared about. Grasp the body of the time, and give it to us. If not, and these men could look at your history, they would say, " This is all very well; we daresay some of these things did happen ; but we were not thinking of these things all day long. It does not represent us."

After enlarging upon this great requisite, imagination, it seems somewhat prosaic to come down to saying that history requires accuracy. But I think I hear the sighs, and sounds more harsh than sighing, of those who have ever investigated anything, and found by dire experience the deplorable inaccuracy which prevails in the world. And, therefore, I would say to the historian almost as the first suggestion, "Be accurate; do not make false references, do not mis-state: and men, if they get no light from you, will not execrate you. You will not stand in the way, and have to be explained and got rid of."

Another most important matter in writing history, and that indeed in which the art lies, is the method of narrating. This is a thing almost beyond rules, like the actual execution in music or painting. A man might have fairness, accuracy, an insight into other times, great knowledge of facts, some power even of arranging them, and yet make a narrative out of it all, so protracted here, so huddled together there, the purpose so buried or confused, that men would agree to acknowledge the merit of the book and leave it unread. There must be a natural line of associations for the narrative to run along. The separate threads of the narrative must be treated separately, and yet the subject not be dealt with sectionally, for that is not the way in which the things occurred. The historian must, therefore, beware that those divisions of the subject which he makes for our ease and convenience, do not induce him to treat his subject in a flimsy manner. He must not make his story easy where it is not so.

After all, it is not by rule that a great history is to be written. Most thinkers agree that the main object for the historian is to get an insight into the things which he tells of, and then to tell them with the modesty of a man who is in the presence of great events; and must speak about them carefully, simply, and with but little of himself or of his affections thrown into the narration.

V. HOW GOOD WRITERS OF HISTORY SHOULD BE CALLED FORTH, AIDED, AND REWARDED.

Mainly by history being properly read. The direct ways of commanding excellence of any kind are very few, if any. When a State has found out its notable men, it should reward them, and will show its worthiness by its measure and mode of reward. But it cannot purchase them. It may do something in the way of aiding them. In history, for instance, the records of a nation may be discreetly managed, and some of the minor work, therefore, done to the hand of the historian. But the most likely method to ensure good historians is to have a fit audience for them. And this is a very difficult matter. In works of general literature, the circle of persons capable of judging is large; even in works of science or philosophy it is considerable: but in history, it is a very confined circle. To the general body of readers, whether the history they read is true or not is in no way perceptible. It is quite as amusing to them when it is told in one way as in another. There is always mischief in error: but in this case the mischief is remote, or seems so. For men of ordinary culture, even if of much intelligence, the difficulty of discerning what is true or false in the histories they read makes it a matter of the highest duty for those few persons who can give us criticism on historical works, at least to save us from insolent and mendacious carelessness in historical writers, if not by just encouragement to secure for nations some results not altogether unworthy of the great enterprise which the writing of history holds out itself to be. " Hujus enim fidei exempla majorum, vicissitudines rerum, fundamenta prudentiæ civilis, hominum denique nomen et fama commissa sunt." *

Ellesmere. Just wait a minute for me, and do not talk about the essay till I come back. I am going for Auster's *Faust.*

Dunsford. What has Ellesmere got in his head?

Milverton. I see. There is a passage where Faust, in his most discontented mood, falls foul of history—in his talk to Wagner, if I am not mistaken.

Dunsford. How beautiful it is this evening! Look at that yellow-green near the sunset.

Milverton. The very words that Coleridge uses. I always think of them when I see that tint.

Dunsford. I daresay his words were in my mind, but I have forgotten what you allude to.

Milverton.

 "O Lady! in this wan and heartless mood,
  To other thoughts by yonder throstle woo'd,
   All this long eve, so balmy and serene,
  Have I been gazing on the western sky,
  And its peculiar tint of yellow-green :
  And still I gaze—and with how blank an eye!

   * Bacon, *de Augmentis Scientiarum.*

And those thin clouds above, in flakes and bars,
That give away their motion to the stars;
Those stars that glide behind them or between,
Now sparkling, now bedimmed, but always seen:
Yon crescent Moon as fixed as if it grew
In its own cloudless, starless lake of blue;
I see them all so excellently fair,
I see, not feel how beautiful they are."

Dunsford. Admirable! In the *Ode to Dejection,* is
it not? where, too, there are those lines,

"O Lady! we receive but what we give,
And in our life alone does Nature live."

Milverton. But here comes Ellesmere with triumph-
ant look. You look as jovial, my dear Ellesmere, as if
you were a Bentley that had found a false quantity in
a Boyle.

Ellesmere. Listen and perpend, my historical friends.

"To us, my friend, the times that are gone by
Are a mysterious book, sealed with seven seals:
That which you call the spirit of ages past
Is but, in truth, the spirit of some few authors
In which those ages are beheld reflected,
With what distortion strange heaven only knows.
Oh! often, what a toilsome thing it is
This study of thine—at the first glance we fly it.
A mass of things confusedly heaped together;
A lumber-room of dusty documents,
Furnished with all approved court-precedents
And old traditional maxims! History!
Facts dramatised say rather—action—plot—
Sentiment, everything the writer's own,

As it bests fits the web-work of his story,
With here and there a solitary fact
Of consequence, by those grave chroniclers,
Pointed with many a moral apophthegm,
And wise old saws, learned at the puppet-shows."

Milverton. Yes; admirable lines; they describe to
the life the very faults we have been considering as the
faults of badly-written histories. I do not see that
they do much more.

Ellesmere.

"To us, my friend, the times that are gone by
Are a mysterious book."—

Milverton. Those two first lines are the full expression of Faust's discontent—unmeasured as in the
presence of a weak man who could not check him.
But, if you come to look at the matter closely, you will
see that the time present is also in some sense a sealed
book to us. Men that we live with daily we often
think as little of as we do of Julius Cæsar, I was going
to say—but we know much less of them than of him.

Ellesmere. I did not mean to say that Faust spoke
my sentiments about history in general. Still, there
are periods of history which we have very few authors
to tell us about, and I daresay in some of those cases
the colouring of their particular minds gives us a false
idea of the whole age they lived in.

Dunsford. This may have happened, certainly.

Milverton. We must be careful not to expect too
much from the history of past ages, as a means of
understanding the present age. There is something

wanted besides the preceding history to understand each age. Each individual life may have a problem of its own, which all other biography accurately set down for us might not enable us to work out. So of each age. It has something in it not known before, and tends to a result which is not down in any books.

Dunsford. Yet history must be of greatest use in discerning this tendency.

Ellesmere. Yes; but the Wagner sort of pedant would get entangled in his round of history—in his historical resemblances.

Dunsford. Now, Milverton, if you were called upon to say what are the peculiar characteristics of this age, what should you say?

Ellesmere. One of Dunsford's questions this, requiring a stout quarto volume with notes in answer.

Milverton. I would rather wait till I was called upon. I am apt to feel, after I have left off describing the character of any individual man, as if I had only just begun. And I do not see the extent of discourse that would be needful in attempting to give the characteristics of an age.

Ellesmere. I think you are prudent to avoid answering Dunsford's question. For my own part, I should prefer giving an account of the age we live in after we have come to the end of it—in the true historical fashion. And so, Dunsford, you must wait for my notions.

Dunsford. I am afraid, Milverton, if you were to write history, you would never make up your mind to condemn anybody.

Milverton. I hope I should not be so inconclusive. I certainly do dislike to see any character, whether of a living or a dead person, disposed of in a summary way.

Ellesmere. For once I will come to the rescue of Milverton. I really do not see that a man's belief in the extent and variety of human character, and in the difficulty of appreciating the circumstances of life, should prevent him from writing history—from coming to some conclusions. Of course such a man is not likely to write a long course of history; but that I hold has been a frequent error in historians—that they have taken up subjects too large for them.

Milverton. If there is as much to be said about men's character and conduct as I think there mostly is, why should we be content with shallow views of them? Take the outward form of these hills and valleys before us. When we have seen them a few times, we think we know them, but are quite mistaken. Approaching from another quarter, it is almost new ground to us. It is a long time before you master the outward form and semblance of any small piece of country that has much life and diversity in it. I often think of this, applying it to our little knowledge of men. Now, look there a moment: you see that house; close behind it is apparently a barren tract. In reality there is nothing of the kind there. A fertile valley with a great river in it, as you know, is between that house and the moors. But the plane of those moors and of the house is coincident from our present point of view. Had we not, as educated men, some distrust of the conclusions of our senses, we should be ready to swear

that there was a lonely house on the border of the
moors. It is the same in judging of men. We see a
man connected with a train of action which is really
not near him, absolutely foreign to him, perhaps, but
in our eyes that is what he is always connected with.
If there were not a Being who understands us immeasurably better than other men can, immeasurably
better than we do ourselves, we should be badly off.

Such precautionary thoughts as these must be useful,
I contend. They need not make us indifferent to
character, or prevent us from forming judgments
where we must form them, but they show us what a
wide thing we are talking about when we are judging
the life and nature of a man.

Ellesmere. I am sure, Dunsford, you are already
convinced : you seldom want more than a slight pretext for going over to the charitable side of things.
You are only afraid of not dealing stoutly enough with
bad things and people. Do not be afraid though. As
long as you have me to abuse, you will say many unjust
things against me, you know, so that you may waste
yourself in good thoughts about the rest of the world,
past and present. Do you know the lawyer's story I
had in my mind then ? " Many times when I have
had a good case," he said, " I have failed ; but then I
have often succeeded with bad cases. And so justice
is done."

Milverton. To return to the subject. It is not a
sort of equalising want of thought about men that I
desire ; only not to be rash in a matter that requires all
our care and prudence.

Dunsford. Well, I believe I am won over. But now to another point. I think, Milverton, that you have said hardly anything about the use of history as an incentive to good deeds and a discouragement to evil ones.

Milverton. I ought to have done so. Bolingbroke gives in his "Letters on History," talking of this point, a passage from Tacitus, " Præcipuum munus annalium,"—can you go on with it, Dunsford ?

Dunsford. Yes, I think I can. It is a passage I have often seen quoted. " Præcipuum munus annalium, reor, ne virtutes sileantur ; utque pravis dictis factisque ex posteritate et infamiâ metus sit."

Ellesmere. Well done ; Dunsford may have invented it, though, for aught that we know, Milverton, and be passing himself off upon us for Tacitus.

Milverton. Then Bolingbroke goes on to say (I wish I could give you his own flowing words), that the great duty of history is to form a tribunal like that amongst the Egyptians which Diodorus tells of, where both common men and princes were tried after their deaths, and received appropriate honour or disgrace. The sentence was pronounced, he says, too late to correct or to recompense ; but it was pronounced in time to render examples of general instruction to mankind. Now, what I was going to remark upon this is, that Bolingbroke understates his case. History well written is a present correction, and a foretaste of recompense, to the man who is now struggling with difficulties and temptations, now overcast by calumny and cloudy misrepresentation.

Ellesmere. Yes; many a man makes an appeal to posterity which will never come before the court; but if there were no such court of appeal——

Milverton. A man's conviction that justice will be done to him in history is a secondary motive, and not one which, of itself, will compel him to do just and great things; but, at any rate, it forms one of the benefits that flow from history, and it becomes stronger as histories are better written. Much may be said against care for fame; much also against care for present repute. There is a diviner impulse than either at the doing of any actions that are much worth doing. As a correction, however, this anticipation of the judgment of history may really be very powerful. It is a great enlightenment of conscience to read the opinions of men on deeds similar to those we are engaged in or meditating.

Dunsford. I think Bolingbroke's idea, which I imagine was more general than yours, is more important: namely, that this judicial proceeding, mentioned by Diodorus Siculus, gave significant lessons to all people, not merely to those who had any chance of having their names in history.

Milverton. Certainly: for this is one of Bolingbroke's chief points, if I recollect rightly.

Ellesmere. Our conversations are much better things than your essays, Milverton.

Milverton. Of course, I am bound to say so: but what made you think of that now?

Ellesmere. Why, I was thinking how in talk we can know exactly where we agree or differ. But I never like to interrupt the essay. I never know when it would come to an end if I did. And so it swims on like a sermon, having all its own way : one cannot put in an awkward question in a weak part, and get things looked at in various ways.

Dunsford. I suppose, then, Ellesmere, you would like to interrupt sermons.

Ellesmere. Why, yes, sometimes—do not throw sticks at me, Dunsford.

Dunsford. Well, it is absurd to be angry with you; because if you long to interrupt Milverton with his cautious perhapses and probablys, of course you will be impatient with discourses which do, to a certain extent, assume that the preacher and the hearers are in unison upon great matters.

Ellesmere. I am afraid to say anything about sermons, for fear of the argumentum baculinum from Dunsford; for many essay writers, like Milverton, delight to wind up their paragraphs with complete little aphorisms—shutting up something certainly, but shutting out something too. I could generally pause upon them a little.

Milverton. Of course one may err, Ellesmere, in too much aphorising as in too much of anything. But your argument goes against all expression of opinion, which must be incomplete, especially when dealing with matters that cannot be circumscribed by exact definitions. Otherwise, a code of wisdom might be made which the fool might apply as well as the wisest man. Even the best proverb, though often the expression of the widest experience in the choicest language, can be

FRIENDS IN COUNCIL.

thoroughly misapplied. It cannot embrace the whole
of the subject, and apply in all cases like a mathematical
formula.   Its wisdom lies in the ear of the hearer.

Ellesmere. Well, I not know that there is anything
more to say about the essay.   I suppose you are aware,
Dunsford, that Milverton does not intend to give us
any more essays for some time.   He is distressing his
mind about some facts which he wants to ascertain
before he will read any more to us.   I imagine we are
to have something historical next.

Milverton. Something in which historical records are
useful.

Ellesmere. Really it is wonderful to see how
beautifully human nature accommodates itself to anything, even to the listening to essays. I shall miss
them.

Milverton. You may miss the talk before and after.

Ellesmere. Well, there is no knowing how much of
that is provoked (provoked is a good word, is it not?)
by the essays.

Dunsford. Then, for the present, we have come to an
end of our readings.

Milverton. Yes, but I trust at no distant time to
have something more to try your critical powers and
patience upon.   I hope that that old tower will yet see
us meet together here on many a sunny day, discussing
various things in friendly council.

www.ingramcontent.com/pod-product-compliance
Lightning Source LLC
Chambersburg PA
CBHW031107020726
47495CB00007B/2092